Jaxson

River Pack Wolves 1

Alisa Woods

Text copyright © 2015 Alisa Woods
All rights reserved.

No part of this publication may be reproduced, stored in a retrieval system, or transmitted in any form or by any means, electronic or mechanical, including photocopying, recording, or otherwise, without written permission from the publisher.

September 2015 Edition
Sworn Secrets Publishing

Cover Design by Steven Novak

ISBN-13: 978-1545190555
ISBN-10: 1545190550

Jaxson (River Pack Wolves 1)
Three brothers. Three Secrets.
One hope to save the shifters in Seattle.

Former SEAL Jaxson River would give his life for his brothers and his pack, but if he doesn't claim a mate soon, he'll be forced to step down as their alpha. There's only one problem: Jaxson's dark secret would kill any mate he claimed. With someone kidnapping shifters off the street—and only Jaxson and his brothers, Jace and Jared, to stop them—now is not the time for his secret to come out.

Curvy Olivia Lilyfield is a half-witch orphan with a dark secret of her own. She wants to atone for it by doing good in the world, so when she finds a wolf being tortured in an alley, she doesn't hesitate to help… even though wolves and witches mix like matches and TNT.

Olivia's dangerous magic means she can't let anyone get too close—but Jaxson can't keep his hands off her, and his kisses are more than she can resist. As they race to save the disappearing shifters of Seattle, the true danger lies in loving each other. They're playing with magical fire… and their secrets could end up destroying them both.

Chapter 1

Olivia stared out the window of her boss's office. The gleaming towers of downtown Seattle looked bright and innocent, but she knew darkness lurked in the corners of the city. Not least in the dingy offices of the local celebrity rag, the *Tales*. Olivia crossed her arms over her chest. There had to be some way out of this assignment.

"Can you do it?" her boss demanded. William Cratchton, editor of the *Tales,* took a long draw on his vape-cigar and puffed out a single noxious plume. He needed to shave off the scraggly salt-and-pepper half-beard before he started looking like a crazy old mountain man.

Olivia unlocked her arms and shook the manila folder of glossy photos clutched in her hand. "Yes, I can do it. I've got a hacker on speed dial who'd love the job. I just was hoping for something a little less... *sleazy*."

A trail of vapor leaked from his smirk. "I pay you for sleaze, Liv."

You hardly pay me at all. But she couldn't afford to voice that thought. In her twenty-five years on the planet, she'd worked every job from barista to pet sitter to a human-sized hot dog advertising some new fast-food place. But she'd never been able to get ahead. Now that she'd finally landed a position in her dream job as a reporter, her finances had just gotten worse. The rent was due. Her phone had been hacked with all kinds of charges she was still paying off. Thank God it was June, and she didn't actually need heat—she was two months past due on that. She really couldn't afford to turn down this assignment.

She held in all her thoughts and went for begging. "What about that story on the homeless shelter I floated last week? There's something rotten there, I'm sure of it. Too much funding and not enough people getting meals..."

JAXSON

"The public's not looking for *righteousness,* Liv." Cratchton gave her a look like she had morphed into a nun before his eyes. "Nobody gives a shit about the homeless. We need naked celebrities to sell copies. Come on, you're a smart girl. You know the score."

This was not what she imagined doing with her life.

Last week, Cratchton had her bribing her way into high-end restaurants with a photographer, just to get a shot of the latest teen hottie out on a date. This week, he wanted her to hack into private cloud accounts for celebrity pictures, hoping to score a sex tape. What next? Actual breaking-and-entering the bedrooms of the rich and glamorous? Where would she draw the line?

Maybe he'd understand if she told him the truth. She softened her voice. "It makes my stomach turn, Bill."

"Yeah, well, give it a few years." He took another draw on his vape. "You'll get used to it."

A sour taste rose up in the back of her throat—he was right. She could feel it getting easier already, like a black ooze that crept in, filling up your lungs more and more until you forgot what clean air felt like. It was easier that way…until, suddenly, it was drowning you.

"I want you on this, Liv. But if you don't want the work…" He put the vape down and leaned forward in his chair. His leering gaze focused on her chest. "We can work out something so you can keep your check this week." He literally licked his lips.

God. Ew.

Her face heated. She crossed her arms over her chest again, and Cratchton's face scrunched in disappointment. She wished she'd worn a turtleneck instead of a button-up blouse that liked to pucker at all the wrong times. She'd always been on the plump side, both ample up top and generous in the hip department, but that only seemed to make her a magnet for lecherous old guys. She ignored Cratchton's surly expression and turned to look out the grimy window of the 14th floor again.

There was darkness in this city, but there was also *goodness*—or at least the potential for it. Good people doing good things, making a difference in the world. *I want to do something that matters with my life.*

"Yeah, well, I'm not paying you to win the Pulitzer."

She blinked and looked back at her boss. She hadn't meant to say that out loud. And she didn't need to win awards—this wasn't about being famous or winning accolades. She just wanted her work to *mean* something.

She'd always been on her own. Ever since her parents died, and she'd spent half her childhood in Seattle's foster care system, bouncing from one lecherous foster-parent to another. All she had wanted was to *survive*. Grow up. Make a difference in the world. She'd couldn't afford the university, but she'd managed to take a few journalism classes at the local community college. She figured she could work her way up... but she didn't count on wading through slime along the way.

Trolling for celebrity sex tapes was even more pathetic, given she was always alone in her own bed. She was too busy working to stay afloat and get the rent paid, all while spending her nights at the public library, trying to teach herself how to be a journalist. There was no time for boyfriends.

Besides, her first boyfriend had cheated on her. And the second one. *He* had wanted a sex tape, too. *Bastard.* She'd kicked him out when she found the other tapes he'd made with a dozen other girls. But she already knew the only person she could really rely on was herself. And with what had happened to her parents... well, it was better if she never fell in love. She wasn't fit to be in a relationship. Not now. Not ever. All she would ever have was her work—and now, even that had been reduced to hacking into the personal lives of celebrities.

"You know what?" She flung the folder at her boss, and the glossies spilled out on the floor. "I'm not doing your dirty work any more, Cratchton."

He scrambled after them, clearly not expecting that response. "Come on, Liv, be smart—"

But she was already halfway to the door, her low heels pounding on the cheap linoleum. She paused in the doorway. "You're a sleazy little mole, Cratchton, chasing sleazy little dollars. I am *not* going to end up like you, sucking down vape and that scotch I know you keep in your drawer. I'm going to do something with my life that *means* something." His face was turning red. She yanked open the door to stop from saying something worse.

"When you come crawling back, don't expect—"

She slammed the door on her way out so she wouldn't have to hear the rest. The drama caught the notice of everyone in the office—which was really just two Cratchtons-in-the-making, only younger and less lecherous, and the girl who hid in her cubicle until someone needed a computer fixed. Olivia had worked there for six months, but she didn't really know any of them. Which was par for the course for her. She didn't bother telling them she wasn't coming back… she just held her head high and marched to the elevator with a glorious *I quit!* expression on her face. She was alone in her triumph on the ride down, and when she reached the street level, she strode out into a burst of rare Seattle sunshine.

It only took a block of striding down the sidewalk before the doubts began to creep in.

What had she done? No assignment meant no check at the end of the week… which meant no rent money. She already had been late a couple times—once more, and her landlord would just toss her out. The churning in her stomach returned with a vengeance. Which only reminded her that she wasn't going to have much in the way of food at the end of the week, either.

She slowed her furious pace. She'd get by somehow—she always had—but she had to admit she'd never pushed it quite this far. Never quit when she had no idea where the next job was coming from. It was a long haul to her apartment on foot, and through a pretty seedy neighborhood as well, but she couldn't afford bus fare now.

She squared her shoulders and kept marching. The walk would give her time to think. Make a plan. Figure out where to start looking for a job, any job, that would hire her right away. Then she could figure out how to do something worthwhile in the world. Something that wouldn't slime her soul.

She glanced at the shops as she passed, looking for *Help Wanted* signs, but most were abandoned in this part of town. Then she realized she was near the homeless shelter—her stomach gave another lurch. She was convinced, from passing it every day on the bus, that something wasn't quite right about the place. Now she had a decent chance of landing there herself. Maybe she could use that—go undercover, find out why there were always people being turned away, like they didn't have enough food or beds or something, even though the place was enormous, a converted warehouse taking up an entire block. And what little research she'd done showed they had tons of money from the government.

It was a great plan—except doing an exposé on the homeless shelter wasn't going to pay the rent. And then she wouldn't have to *pretend* to be homeless. She sighed and came to a stop at the end of the long storefront of the shelter. The street was empty, and now that her heels weren't clacking on the concrete, she heard a strange electric twitching sound, like something was shorting out. Then a low groan.

Her heart thudded. The groan turned into a grunt, then the sound of something hitting the pavement… and then a soul-breaking whimper. Her legs were locked in place—the sound was coming from the alley just ahead, a darkened space between the shelter and the next concrete building.

Something very bad was happening there.

Her legs shook, but she managed to make them move. She edged forward until she was just at the corner of the alley. The crackling continued, and her stomach jumped with it like it was filled with a hundred electrified butterflies. But she forced herself into the open so she could see down the long, shadowed alley.

What she saw made ice run through her veins.

JAXSON

There were two men at the end, dressed in black fatigues and boots, holding long metal sticks with blue electric arcs at the tip—and they were torturing an animal. It whimpered and writhed on the grimy pavement, just beyond an overflowing dumpster and before a boarded-up chain-link fence. They kept jabbing and jabbing it, darting in close then backing up as the animal snapped at them.

It was a wolf.

She froze. This was no ordinary wolf—if such a thing could even manage to wander into downtown Seattle. It was massive, easily the size of a man, with shiny black fur bristled out and fangs larger than her hand. It had to be a shifter—and the men were torturing it with their cattle prods.

Olivia swallowed down her fear, edged farther into the alley, and fumbled to get her phone out of the pocket of her skirt. Shifters were dangerous—they were just one of the magical creatures that lived in the shadows of Seattle, and she knew exactly how deadly the supernatural could be. But no matter how dangerous shifters might be, she knew there was a human being inside. And anyone torturing a shifter in an alley was probably worse than the shifter itself.

Besides, she couldn't stand by and let them kill someone in front of her.

Her hand was shaking, but she managed to swipe her phone on and start recording. Somehow the small ding of the video caught the men's attention, even over the sparking of their torture sticks and the growling of the beast. They whipped their heads to look at her, then at each other.

Her heart nearly leaped out of her chest, but she mustered up a strong voice anyway. "I've called the police!" she lied. "And I've got you on camera. Just put the sticks down, and they'll go easy on you." *God, what was she doing?*

The attackers seemed to think the same thing. But in their distraction, the shifter leaped up and snapped at one of them. The beefier man jabbed the shifter in the face with the prod, while the more slender one turned toward her and started sprinting down the alley, stick in hand.

Oh shit.

Olivia stood her ground. "I'm recording this!" Her voice squeaked—that didn't do anything to slow the man down. She should run… she *wanted* to run… but her legs were turning to jelly underneath her. Just as the man reached out a hand to grab her still-extended phone, a blur of fur and snapping jaws flashed between them. The man and wolf both slammed against the brick wall and bounced back off again. The man screamed as the wolf clamped its jaws onto him. Olivia skittered out of the path of the rolling, fighting, clawing ball of man and beast. She plastered herself against the cool brick wall, out of the way.

It was quickly over—the shifter had the man pinned with his throat in its jaws. Blood was smeared on his arm, but not at his neck. The second man, the bigger one, had raced down the alley to help his partner, but the shifter let loose a growl that raised all the hairs on the back of Olivia's neck... and that sound stopped the second man in his tracks. With one bite, the shifter could snap the downed man's neck. But instead, it growled a second warning. The man who was standing finally got it—he dropped his torture stick and held up his hands. The shifter slowly released its grip on the first man's throat. Then it let loose one of those bone-chilling growls right in the man's face, spittle and foam dropping onto his terrified, pale cheeks. He didn't move a muscle until the shifter slowly backed away. Then both men scrambled to run from the alleyway. When they were gone, the wolf loped back toward the dumpster and disappeared behind it.

Olivia's heart was pounding in her chest, her phone was still gripped in her hand. She tapped it to stop recording and tried to catch her breath, which was raging out of control. She should leave—hustle her stupid-stupid self right out of the alley while she could—but she didn't trust her legs. She was quivering head-to-toe, and only managed to stay upright because the brick wall was holding her up. Just as her heaving breaths started to calm, the sound of rapid footsteps scraping the pavement drew her attention back down the alley.

The most gorgeous man she'd ever seen was hurrying toward her.

It had to be the shifter—and he was even more massive as a man than he had been as a wolf. Tall and built like a mountain. Broad shoulders with muscles that flexed as he pulled a t-shirt over his head. Words were tattooed across his chest, but she couldn't read them before they disappeared under his ragged t-shirt. She could still see his ripped abs through the holes and all the way down to his still-unbuttoned jeans. She yanked her gaze back up. His hair was black-as-midnight, just like his fur coat, and it gleamed in the sunshine finally pushing back the shadows of the alley.

He was undeniably hot, but he was *rushing* at her, and he was still a *shifter*. Olivia unlocked her quivering body and scrambled to grab one of the cattle-prod sticks the men had left behind. She held it in front of her to ward off the shifter and shrunk back against the wall.

He jogged to a stop just out of her reach. "Whoa! Hey…" He raised both hands into the air. "I'm not going to hurt you. Promise." He gave her a lopsided smile that sent flutters through her lady parts, but she kept the stick trained on him.

"You're a *shifter*," she said, stating the obvious because her brain was blurry from everything that had happened.

"And you're a *human*," he said with a laugh in his voice. "I figured that out on account of an electric prod being your weapon of choice."

Damn. Even his voice was drenched in hotness. And he was only partly right about her being human, but she certainly wasn't going to point that out. Her hand was shaking, but she managed to keep him at a distance with the stick.

He relaxed his hands-up position. "Come on, now. You're not going to hurt me with that thing." He extended one hand toward her, palm up. "How about you just give it to me, we put it down, and we can call this whole thing done?" He edged a little closer, slowly reaching for the cattle prod like she was a skittish but heavily-armed deer, all while holding her gaze with gorgeous clear blue eyes as bright as the Seattle sky.

Her hand wavered, but who was she kidding? This man wasn't going to hurt her. She let out a shuddering breath and handed the torture stick over to him. His face lit with a smile, and he tossed the cattle prod behind him, sending it clattering on the pavement. Hands now free, he dropped them to work at the buttons on his pants. He was standing far too close, and it was clear he was going commando underneath his tattered jeans. She swallowed and tried to look anywhere else other than the gorgeous man dressing in front of her.

Her desperate attempt didn't go unnoticed. "Sorry," he said, drawing her back. "Nudity is an occupational hazard." His smile had morphed into a full smirk. "And you've got to be kidding me, trying to stop those guys with a phone." He nodded to the device in her hand, which was now hanging limp at her side.

"I… um…" God, why wouldn't her mouth work? Oh right. Because a Greek God was standing in front of her and… *was he checking her out?* His gaze was roaming her body, scouring and scrutinizing every inch.

"Are you all right?" he asked, his gaze finally reaching hers again.

Her cheeks flamed. He was just *concerned* about her, not hot for her too-plump body. *Obviously.* She was embarrassed she'd even conjured that thought. Had to be leftover tremors still rattling her brain.

She swallowed and managed to find her voice. "I'm fine." But her voice squeaked, and he frowned in response.

He looked her over again, and then slowly leaned in to plant his hands on either side of her head, surrounding her with a mountain of muscles. She sucked in a breath and pressed harder against the wall. He wasn't touching her, but she could feel the warmth radiating from his muscular arms. The scent of pine, warm earth, and the heat of the fight was on him. She should be terrified, struggling to get away, but instead she was overwhelmed by the raw sex-appeal rolling off him in waves.

"You're not all right," he said softly, peering into her eyes. "You're in shock. You just witnessed a violent attack in an alley with dangerous men you don't know. I'm sorry you had to see that, but it's over now. You're safe. And I promise I won't let any harm come to you." He dipped his head, leaning even closer. "Do you believe me?"

She nodded, somewhat erratically. But she actually *did* believe him—he could obviously kill her if he wanted, but instead, he was reassuring her. With his words. And his body. And his ridiculously sexy voice.

His smile returned, and he eased back a little, but still stayed close enough to make her chest hurt with how hard her heart was pounding.

"Thanks for trying to save me," he said, voice still soft. "That was a very sweet thing to do. Brave and sweet. Also very stupid."

She gave a small shrug, as much as she could with him so close. Because what could she do, walk away? "They were going to kill you." His nearness was making it hard for her to breathe. Hard to speak.

His smile blazed brighter. "Actually, I had just gotten them right where I wanted them."

That made her eyebrows hike up. "It didn't quite look that way from this end of the alley."

"You'll just have to trust me on that." The smirk was almost too much, especially this close, but then it faded. He leaned in fast and planted a light kiss on her cheek. "But thank you anyway," he whispered in her ear.

Her breath hitched, and goosebumps ran races up and down her body.

She expected him to pull away, but instead, he seemed to be drawing in a breath with his lips still near her cheek. *Was he scenting her?* She had heard shifter wolves could do that—smell far more than any normal human. And maybe hear things, too. God, she prayed he didn't smell the wetness pooling between her legs. When he finally pulled back, he peered at her, frowning. Like he had an unspoken question and was searching for the answer in her eyes.

"Can I kiss you?" His voice was soft and wondering.

What? "I think you just did." She really, *really* couldn't breathe.

His smirk blazed to life again. *"That* wasn't even close to a kiss."

Then he closed the few inches between them and

pressed his lips to hers. They were strong and soft and hungry for her. His hands cupped her cheeks, lifting her away from the wall and angling her so his lips could demand more. A fire burst to life inside her, a burning heat that traveled straight from her mouth to between her legs. And when his tongue asked permission to taste her, she opened for him without thinking. He plunged in and kissed her so deeply and thoroughly that her legs gave out entirely—only his hand around her waist, pressing her body to his, kept her upright. When he eased back from the kiss, his breath was hot on her face, and his eyes were wide.

She was panting like she'd run a mile. Her body ached with the need for more. The last thing she wanted was for him to let go… but he did. His frown grew like he wasn't sure what to make of her, or their kiss, or something.

He stepped back and held her at arm's length, eyeing her shaky legs. "Can you stand?"

"I am quite capable of standing, thank you." His smirk made her heated skin flame even more. She straightened her blouse, which was rumpled from the kiss. It was obvious how much effect he'd had on her. And that she hadn't had anywhere near the same effect on him.

But she couldn't help the thrill that ran through her body when he took her arm to support her. He gently shuffled them toward the street, then slid his hand down, taking her phone and lacing his fingers with hers. He blazed a smile that banished her embarrassment and tilted his head down the street.

"Why don't you hail us a cab?" he asked.

It seemed a peculiar request—and besides, she couldn't afford a cab—yet having his hand locked with hers steadied her. And somehow filled her with a sense of safety. So she raised her hand and signaled a distant yellow car. It took a while for it to amble over. When it arrived, the gorgeous man on her arm opened the door and gestured for her to step in. Then he leaned forward and produced a wad of bills from his tattered jeans to give to the driver.

"Take her home. And make sure she's safely inside before you leave." His voice was full of authority now. He glanced at the cabby's license. "Markus Trenton, cab license number 4523974. If anything happens to her, I'll be tracking you down and holding you personally accountable. Are we clear?"

The cabby's eyes went wide, but he took the outstretched money. "Sure, man. Whatever you want."

Then the shifter turned his blazing blue eyes on her and smiled. "Don't do any more stupid things, camera girl." He closed the door of the cab before she could protest.

JAXSON

It whisked away from the curb. She sat there, stunned. He had sent her off by herself. And somehow had money for a cab, even though his clothes were full of holes, like the homeless men in the shelter. It wasn't until a minute or two later that she realized... the shifter still had her phone.

Of course. She cursed loud enough that the cabbie glanced in the rear-view mirror at her. Mr. Hot Shifter had wanted her phone. The rest—the soft words, the heated kiss—was all just a diversion. She slumped back against the seat. Now she was out a job *and* a phone.

But that scorching hot kiss...

She gingerly touched her fingers to her lips. They were still swollen.

That almost made it all worthwhile.

Chapter 2

The shower and fresh clothes didn't erase her scent from his mind.

Not that Jaxson really wanted them to. His inner wolf was still sulking that he hadn't followed up that blazing-hot kiss with something more substantial... and long-lasting. His beast would never understand what the man in him knew all too well—there would never be a mate for either of them. But it hadn't been his wolf that had drunk in the sweet lips of that gorgeously curvy brunette in the alley. That was all on him.

And he was a fool for doing it.

JAXSON

Jaxson propped his feet on his desk, the bright Seattle morning making glare spots on the polished wood. He had ignored his brother Jace's concerned looks on the way in and slammed the door to his private office behind him. Hopefully, that would hold off the debriefing on his failed mission while he sorted out this thing with the girl.

Why was he—and his wolf—so drawn to her?

Jaxson swiped open her phone for the tenth time... then swiped it off again. He shouldn't rifle through her information. He should just delete the video, get enough to track down her address, and mail her phone back. As lead alpha of the River pack, and CEO of Riverwise, the private security business he shared with his two brothers, he had bucketloads of responsibilities on a normal day—never mind a failed mission, and the heat he was coming under to find a mate.

He didn't have time for a mysterious girl.

If only she didn't taste so damn good.

But that wasn't really it—he'd had plenty of human girls. They were fun, but their skin had never sizzled his lips with some kind of hot magic when he kissed them. His wolf had never howled like it was being ripped apart when he sent one packing in a cab.

This girl was different. He just didn't know *why*.

Jaxson swiped open the phone again and watched the video she took. He had to admit it looked pretty bad from her angle. Which only made him wince... but he had to put in a good performance or there was no way he'd infiltrate the operation going on at the homeless shelter. As bad as the video looked, the girl's hand was remarkably steady with the camera. A grin stretched his face as her words shouted at him from the phone. *I've called the police! And I've got you on camera.* World-class bluffing from a girl with luscious curves and a smart mouth.

Okay, he could understand why the *man* in him would be attracted—but why had his wolf raged against his skin, demanding that he claim her right then and there in the alley? Jaxson scowled at the video, stopping it, then deleting it. If his wolf thought he had found their mate, then that was just one more reason to toss the phone and never look back. This brave, amazing girl didn't deserve to get mixed up in his messy life... or his fate.

He dropped the phone in the wastebasket by his desk.

It stayed there for a full ten seconds before he pulled it out again.

Dammit.

He flipped through her pictures. No selfies, unfortunately. Just a bunch of shots of a restaurant and some guy with a professional-grade camera. Was she doing surveillance? Jaxson immediately disliked the cameraman—not least because he was reasonably good-looking and smiling way too hard for her picture. *For her.* His wolf snarled with a completely unreasonable jealousy. Jaxson was glad there was only the one shot of the guy.

The rest were pictures of the sunset over the bay, a couple seagulls, and an almost artistic shot from the inside of a room with a glass-and-steel-gridded roof. The orange glow of the setting sun had set the panes on fire, making a magical light show splash across the room. It took him a moment to figure it out, but he was pretty sure it was the Seattle Public Library.

The library. So she visits the library, does surveillance on the side, and tries to rescue tortured shifters in alleys.

Who *was* this girl?

A quick search brought up her name—Olivia Lilyfield—but practically no other personal information. It was almost like this was a burn phone. Her address book was nearly blank, but two of the entries were very illuminating. Cratchton at the *Tales.* Google said he was the editor. And the second—listed as Mark—had the cameraman picture as his profile. The third was simply listed at Xenon. No picture. Local number.

Cameraman. The *Tales.* So she's a reporter. Even more reason to stay away... and yet, his fingers were itching to dial the number at the celebrity rag to see if he could track her down. Just to hear her voice. Make sure she got back okay.

Only he sent her home, not to the office. And there was no record of a home address on the phone. A simple search online would bring it up... he was already tapping out the search request when Jace flung open the door.

His brother let the door bang against the wall, then leaned against the doorjamb with his arms crossed, glaring at him. Jace was younger by two years, but he became an alpha in his own right when he joined the army as a medic. His time overseas was... mixed. Jace had served his country well, but the scars he brought home were the kind that didn't show on the outside... and that no one had yet been able to heal. Not that Jaxson hadn't tried.

"Are you ready to admit what a tremendously bad idea that was?" Jace asked smugly. "Because I've got ten dollars riding on this, and it's time Jared lost a bet." Their older brother was a notoriously bad loser. Which only meant Jace took it as a personal challenge to have him lose as often as possible.

Jaxson was glad he had already erased the video. He stood and slid the phone into his pocket. "I didn't get to find out. Got interrupted before I could get in."

Jace frowned. "Interrupted?" He ran a quick look over Jaxson. "You're still walking. Couldn't have been too bad." Shifters healed quickly, but he'd been gone less than an hour. "What happened?"

JAXSON

Jaxson sighed as he walked around the desk to face Jace. He crossed his arms and leaned back against it. "Doesn't matter. What *does* matter is that we're no closer to getting inside. And the clock is ticking, Jace."

"Yeah, I know." His brother ran a hand over the scruff on his face, which made Jaxson wince. Another sleepless night, rolling out of bed to stumble into the office. Jace couldn't keep going like this. But they had other problems they had to solve first.

"I can try going back in," Jaxson said, "but not yet. It would be too suspicious if I showed up the next day, offering myself up for capture again. You may be right. We might have to tackle this head-on with a straight-up assault."

His brother arched an eyebrow. "Jared will be pleased to hear you've finally come to your senses."

Jaxson shook his head. It was risky, but he was running out of options. "When's he getting back from the mountains?" Their older brother had taken the rest of the pack out to the Olympic Mountains for the weekend—for tactical training, weapons practice, the usual. Only with Jared as their CO, Jaxson was sure everyone would be limping into the office on Monday. If not outright taking a sick day to heal up at home.

"On Friday, he said would be in for interviews this afternoon." Jace shrugged. They both knew Jared kept his own schedule. He had a darkness of his own to carry, one that no one could ever fix. Jace and Jaxson had long ago stopped talking about it—that was the only way they could keep Jared with them, and not have him end up a feral shifter anarchist in Idaho. They'd never see him again.

"Wait... interviews?" Jaxson asked, frowning. "Has Jared decided to bring on a secretary?" He had hoped the paperwork might keep Jared engaged, spending more time in the office where they could keep an eye on him. But apparently not.

"Office assistant." Jace made air quotes. "But yeah. I guess he decided it wasn't so easy running payroll after all." Jace smirked—that had been his job before Jared decided the youngest River brother was too incompetent to cut checks and invoice clients. Since then, Jared had done nothing but complain about pushing paper instead of running drills or spending time on the firing range. He was a sharpshooter during his time in the Marines, and that was where he spent most of his downtime.

Which really wasn't good for anyone.

"This is the first I've heard that we're hiring." Jaxson held in the growl. "Who are we interviewing?"

"Humans." Clearly Jace thought this was a mistake.

Jaxson did, too. *"What?* Did he just forget we're an undercover shifter operation? Or that our clients are very sensitive about their personal information?" Riverwise Private Security had an A-list of clients that was very black-book. The rich and infamous of Seattle's bustling new dot com celebrities understood very well how easily they could be exposed. And they entrusted Riverwise to keep that from happening. "What about Thea? She's got a background in accounting, right?"

"Thea?" Jace looked like he was about to choke on his spit. "The hot daughter of the alpha of the Blue Mountain pack? I thought you had your eye on that smokin' redhead in the Northern pack? She's shopping for a mate now, you know. You better make your move, or you'll get aced out."

"We're not talking about a mate." Jaxson's growl definitely leaked into his voice this time. "We're talking about a secretary."

"Office assistant." Jace's grin was a mile wide.

Jaxson bared his fangs.

Jace just laughed. But he quickly reeled it in. "Jaxson, come on." He held out his hands, imploring. "You know how it works. You bring Thea in here, and everyone's going to think you're looking to finally settle down. We've got three packs we could be making alliances with, and we can't afford to piss off any of them. We need all the help we can get. Especially if we're going to start doing direct assaults."

"Yeah, I know." This was not where he wanted the conversation to go. Jaxson slipped his hand into his pocket, running a thumb over the phone's face. *Olivia.* Her name rolled around in his mind, sparking all kinds of feelings he had no right to have. Especially for a human.

Only... maybe she wasn't. If not, she was even more dangerous to have around. But the mere possibility had his wolf sitting up and demanding they go after her. Jaxson studied the carpet in front of him, trying to decide just how big a fool he actually was. Returning the phone personally was a really bad idea. Probably why he was considering it.

"Earth to Jaxson." Jace was waving a hand in front of his face.

Christ. He was such a mess.

Jaxson batted his hand away and growled.

Jace just leaned back and frowned. "What's going on?"

"It's nothing," he said, taking his hand off the phone and out of his pocket.

"You can't dodge it forever, Jaxson. You're almost thirty. If you don't take a mate, people are going to assume you're like Jared."

"I'm not *broken,* Jace." Not like that, at least.

"Yeah. I... *know that.*" His brother frowned even deeper like he hadn't questioned it before, but now he

JAXSON

wondered. And Jaxson couldn't afford for Jace to get suspicious—because his brother was too smart, and he would figure it out eventually.

Jaxson just glared at him.

Jace let out a frustrated sigh. "Man, I'm the last to push you into this, but you know the situation. The pack needs an alpha—a *mated* alpha, a leader to bring us all together—and you're it. We need you, especially now. And the pack needs an alliance if we're going to accomplish all the things we want. You know we can't do all of this just with the River pack."

"I know." Frustration clipped his words.

"So figure out which of the hot, eligible female wolves out there floats your boat and *claim her*... now, before not having a mate tears down everything we've worked for."

Jaxson rubbed a hand across his forehead. The pounding was getting steadier. "I just need a little more time, Jace. To figure this out." He had no solution; he knew that. It was just postponing the inevitable—the day he let down his brothers, his pack, and countless other shifters for good.

"Hey." Jace strode over to put a hand on Jaxson's shoulder. His grip was tight, but he looked like he was making an effort to lighten things up. "I don't want to pressure you, man. If I could take on the burden of mating with the hottest female wolf out there, I would.

Maybe I could trial run a few for you."

Jaxson shoved away his brother's hand, but he couldn't help the grin. "Shut up."

Jace grinned and held his hands up in surrender, backing up. "Just saying... there are worse fates, bro."

That killed Jaxson's smile. Because he knew Jace and Jared would trade places with him in a heartbeat, if they could. Each had their own dark reasons for not being able to take a mate. Which only meant that carrying on the line fell to him... not to mention leading the pack and making alliances. All of it was his responsibility, and they would see no reason for him not to uphold it. But that was only because they didn't know he had already failed them years ago.

"So what's our new plan?" Jace asked, thankfully circling back to the mission.

"I'll have one by the time Jared comes in." Jaxson's hand slipped into his pocket again without his bidding. The phone was still warm from when he held it before. "I'll be back for the interviews as well. I've got some business to attend to first."

Jace gave him a knowing smirk, probably thinking he was finally getting busy with finding a mate. But his brother couldn't be more wrong—Jaxson was going to return the phone and clean up that mess so he could focus on finding a way to clean up all the others.

Chapter 3

Olivia really wished she had her phone.

She could use the library's computers to submit online applications, as well as search for local jobs that might float the rent, but how was she supposed to check email? Or even use the GPS to find these places? If an employer wanted to reach her, it wasn't like they could call her. She'd applied to ten positions so far—from bank teller to office assistant to donut maker—but all of them wanted a phone number for interviews. Even with email, she couldn't camp out at the library all day, every day, hoping for a reply.

Shoving all the worries aside, Olivia dove into another fifteen-page application form.

"Looks like hard work," a deeply sexy voice said from behind her.

She jolted in her seat, pounding the table hard enough to send the cup of tiny pencils tumbling. Masculine hands reached past her to right the cup, then the owner of the voice moved into her field of view and leaned against the computer table, facing her.

It was the shifter.

She scooted her chair back in surprise, and her heart lurched. "What are you doing here?"

"Well, I tried your office, but it seems you don't work there anymore." He looked a little worried about that. "And the cabbie said he brought you here instead of taking you home."

"So… you're stalking me now?" His sudden appearance rattled her. She did *not* need any more drama in this day.

"No!" he protested. Then the frown deepened as he dropped his gaze. "Well, yes, actually." He held out his hand—it was her phone! "You'd probably like this back."

She slowly leaned forward in her chair to pluck the phone from his outstretched hand. Then she scooted the chair back a little, afraid he might change his mind and take it back.

He grimaced. "Look, I'm sorry about that—"

"Why did you take it?" She already had it open, but it looked the same as before. Two swipes verified what she suspected: he had deleted the video.

"I just wanted to make sure—"

"You could have asked."

"Excuse me?"

"You could have asked." She looked up at him, defiant. "I would have deleted the video in front of you. There was no need to take the phone."

His shoulders dropped. "You're right. I'm sorry."

That mollified her. Slightly. Plus he had changed into slim-fitting dress pants and a white collared shirt that both seemed tailored to perfectly fit his sculpted muscles. He was ridiculously good-looking in tattered jeans—in these sexy, high-end clothes, she was having a hard time keeping her eyes from traveling the length of his body.

He dipped his chin and captured her with those gorgeous sky-blue eyes. "The truth is, I wanted to... well, I wanted to know more about you." He seemed to be asking her forgiveness with this, but why would a gorgeous guy like him, obviously much better off than she was and a shifter besides, want to know more about her? She was nobody.

She scooted her chair toward him, but only so she could tap her computer screen awake again. It was about to time her out. When she looked up, he had moved closer to peer at her screen. Her face flushed, but he already knew she was out of a job. The scent of him—fresh pines and heated earth—washed over her again, reminding her of that blazing kiss in the alleyway.

Before she could scoot back again, out of the zone of his overwhelming hotness, he reached out to her, like he wanted to shake hands. "Can we start over? My name's Jaxson River. I'm very pleased to make your acquaintance."

His gaze held hers, and his formal tone compelled a small smile onto her face. "Olivia Lilyfield, unemployed reporter. Nice to meet you." She slipped her hand into his... and almost pulled back. There was something about his touch that instantly brought her entire body to life—almost like tiny pleasure-shocks racing down to her toes, up through her core, and straight to her heart. Her breath caught. And he wasn't letting go of her hand—instead he covered it with his other one and dropped to one knee in front of her.

His eyes were wide. "I have to ask you something." His voice was a little breathless, and in spite of his words, he seemed to be holding back.

"What?" The sensation of him holding her hand so gently between his was heating every part of her—like he was a live wire, and just touching him was igniting small

JAXSON

brush fires inside her.

He dropped his voice low and leaned even closer. "Are you a shifter? You already know my secret. Trust me that you're safe in telling me yours."

She shook her head in tiny motions. "No."

"Are you certain?" he pressed. "Maybe you're only half. Maybe you haven't expressed yet, but your father or mother was a shifter—"

She pulled her hand from his and shrunk back in the chair. "My parents are dead."

"Oh." He looked pained. "I'm sorry, Olivia, I… I didn't realize."

"It happened a long time ago," she said stiffly. And her mother was definitely not your average mom—she was a witch. Olivia knew all too well that she had inherited some of her mother's command of the supernatural. But there was no way she was telling this shifter any of that… no matter how hot he was or how sexy his voice. She kept her distance from the supernatural world as much as possible, but she still understood the basics—including the legendary blood feuds between witches and wolves. Or really witches and any kind of shifter. She didn't know if her mother ever partook of the dark arts she'd heard of, but she knew for sure that shifters and witches were natural enemies. And the soft look on this shifter's face—his name was Jaxson, she reminded herself—would evaporate in a second if he knew what she was.

Even if she was only half witch.

His gaze was roaming her face. "I'm sorry for probing." His voice was soft, apologetic. "My inner wolf and I were having a disagreement." He gave a small smile, and she was sure a part of her was melting inside. Why did he have to be so sexy?

"A disagreement about what?" she asked.

He motioned her closer, tugging on the arm of her chair to roll it an inch or two forward, just enough that he could lean in to whisper in her ear. "My wolf thinks I should be dragging you off to a dark corner of the library and running my paws all over you."

Her heart lurched with his sexy words whispering against her skin. A shiver literally ran up her back. She pulled away to look into his eyes. "But you disagree." Damn, it was hot in here. *Was he really saying this to her?*

He dropped his gaze to her chest, the buttoned shirt still inconveniently puckering. Then he slowly drew a hot line with his gaze as he worked his way back up to her face. His grin was wicked and sexy and was igniting her nether regions. "Oh no, we definitely agree about that part."

She swallowed. "I see." Not that she did, but she was having trouble forming words.

"The thing is, my wolf is convinced you're a shifter. A wolf shifter to be precise. He insisted we come back and find out, because he really, really wants it to be true."

Is that what he wanted? A shifter to get hot and heavy with? It made sense for a shifter to want to be with their own kind. "I'm sorry to disappoint him." And at that moment, she kind of wished she could have been—at least for a quick tryst in the stacks. That would certainly redeem this hellacious day.

"You're sure you're not?" he asked again.

"Afraid so."

But instead of looking disappointed, he seemed a little relieved by her answer. She wasn't sure how to feel about that. He straightened up from the floor and leaned against the library table, thankfully giving her room to breathe again. Although she instantly missed his closeness even as she was glad to be released from the intensity.

He glanced at her computer screen—it had gone dark while they talked. "You're looking for a new job."

She pulled in a breath and tried to regain some dignity. "Yes. The last one was... well, morally challenged."

He blazed a smile. "Maybe you could help me out with something."

She lifted an eyebrow. "You mean, other than saving you in the alley?"

His face fell into a frown. "I had that under control."

"And not reporting you for phone theft?" She enjoyed the small squirm he did on the table.

"I was just borrowing it."

"I see."

"Okay, okay." He held up his hands. "Ms. Olivia Lilyfield, I need your help, and I'm willing to pay you for it."

That got her attention. The smirk fell off her face. "What do you mean?"

The smile was back on his face, although gentler this time. "My brothers and I run a private security firm. Riverwise—maybe you've heard of it?"

Heard of it? They only handled the most prestigious, and secretive, clients in the Seattle Metro area. "I might have heard you mentioned in the *Tales* once or twice."

He gave her a scowl, but it seemed mostly teasing. "It so happens, we're in need of a secretary, er... office assistant."

"Really?" Her pulse quickened. Was he actually offering her a job?

"I think you're just what we need... under one condition."

Her shoulders slumped. "What?" God, if it was something sleazy, she was just going to give up on this day and go home and eat ice cream. All night.

JAXSON

"Well… it's kind of embarrassing. And a bit awkward." He looked genuinely uncomfortable—which just intrigued her.

"Well, if you were doing your job in stalking me, you should know that I specialize in embarrassing and awkward."

He let out a short laugh, and the smile was back on his face. She really liked it much better that way. His smoldering hot looks made her panties dampen, but this look—this *smile*—seemed like it was an infrequent visitor to his face. Like there were more dark clouds than sunshine in his life. And for some reason that made her heart hurt, even though she really shouldn't have any feelings whatsoever for this man. Beyond the obvious. Any woman with a pulse would lust after Jaxson River.

He was studying her face, his expression growing serious. Then he dropped to one knee and drew close to her again. "Here's the thing," he said, taking a breath and letting it out slow. "I need a mate."

Her eyebrows hiked up. "A mate?" It was a shifter thing, mating for life. Some kind of magic that bound them together—that was about all she knew.

"Yes. It's expected. I'm alpha of my pack, and I'm supposed to take a mate to solidify my leadership position. And, if possible, mate with one of the daughters of a rival pack. To form an alliance of sorts."

"But you don't want to?" she guessed. That had to be it, because she couldn't imagine in a million years why Jaxson River couldn't have any woman he wanted—shifter or otherwise, for one night or forever.

"It's not that I don't want to." He bit his lip. There was a weird sort of dance of emotions across his face. Whatever he was about to tell her, she had a feeling there was more behind it than whatever words he was carefully choosing in his head. "I'd very much like to have a mate," he said finally, and that had the ring of truth. "I'm just not ready for it yet. Even though everyone else seems to think I should be."

"Sounds like kind of a sticky problem."

"It is." He seemed relieved like maybe he expected her to judge him for not wanting to be magically bound to someone forever. She'd pretty much given up on "forever-type" relationships—they just weren't in the cards for her—so she could understand. The world didn't like it when you weren't paired up with someone. Or at least wanted to be.

She put her hand on his, meaning to reassure him, but there was that weird sensation again—like touching him was waking up something inside her. She pulled back, using words instead. "I'm not much the mating type myself."

He frowned at this. "You're not?"

She shrugged. "Lost my parents early. Did years of duty tour through foster care. Had a couple disastrous boyfriends. Let's just say, I understand the choice of staying single. Being in a relationship isn't meant for everyone."

His frown carved deeper. "Do you think you can be happy that way? I mean long-term. Without someone as a mate, er, I guess husband, in your case?" His earnest look was so sweet, so genuinely curious, she didn't take any offense to it.

But it still made her shy. "Yeah. I mean, I hope so. My work is important to me."

He glanced at the computer screen, confusion on his face.

"I'm still figuring that part out." She could feel the edge of defensiveness creep into her voice.

"I see." And strangely, it seemed like he did.

She relaxed the hunch in her shoulders.

A smile slowly grew on his face. "Olivia Lilyfield, I think you're *exactly* what I needed to find today."

"Come again?" Her face scrunched up.

He stood and offered a hand up from the stool she was perched on. She took it, even though every time she touched him just reminded her how much she *really* wouldn't mind a quick tumble in the sheets with Jaxson River. Maybe that was still on the table if he wasn't really looking for a mate. Then again, why in the world would he want to sneak off to the stacks with an overly curvy ex-reporter, possible secretary? It didn't make any sense.

"Riverwise needs an office assistant." His smile was confident again. "I need someone to help me manage the pressures of acquiring a mate. And you..." He tapped her nose with his finger in a way that made her blush. "... you need a job that means something. I think we can work something out to our mutual benefit."

She bit her lip. "My rent's due at the end of the week. Any chance of a check by then?"

He blazed a smile. "Absolutely no problem."

She sighed, and the tension she'd been carrying since she strode out of the *Tales* office finally seeped out of her body. "Then, Mr. Jaxson River, looks like you've found your new office assistant."

He tucked her hand around his arm and led her out of the library.

Chapter 4

Jaxson's wolf was yipping in happy circles inside him. All because he was bringing Olivia back to the office. Of course, his wolf thought that meant they would soon be bending her over his desk and finding out just how luscious those curves really were... Jaxson sucked in a breath and held the frosted-glass door of Riverwise open for Olivia. He really had to stop thinking of her that way, no matter how much his wolf—and he—wanted that little fantasy to play out.

Everything he said to Olivia was true—she needed a job, Riverwise needed an assistant, and he needed someone to help him work this sticky mess of delaying a mate as long as possible. But even more, he was intrigued by the electric touches... her smart mouth... and what was this about her not wanting a husband? There was something wrong there. Something deep and dark and sorrowful in those chocolate brown eyes. And it was killing him not to know what it was.

Bringing her into the office meant he could keep her close. Spend more time with her. Maybe figure out where that dark sorrow was coming from. But he could already tell: the more time he spent with her, the more he wanted. And not just because his wolf was drooling for her.

In his preoccupation with Olivia, he had forgotten Jared was conducting interviews this afternoon. His brother was in the main conference room—which was simply the open space in the center of the office. The three River brothers, along with the rest of the pack, had their offices around the perimeter, but they conducted all their meetings in the breezy open space in the middle. Jared was sitting there now, grilling a thin girl who appeared barely old enough to vote. With Jared's oversized bulk, rolled up sleeves, and camouflage pants, he was barraging her with questions. His boots were still muddy from the weekend in the Olympics. Jaxson could see the interviewee's slender fingers shake from halfway across the room.

He rubbed a hand across his forehead. Why hadn't he seen this coming?

"We'll have to do a background check on you, of course. Better if you tell us up front *now* about any illegal drug use, contraband smuggling, compromising affairs—"

"Jared?" Jaxson put enough point in his voice to interrupt his brother.

He threw a scowl at Jaxson, then pressed on, ignoring him. "Compromising affairs could be virtually any liaison with a foreign national, someone in cyber security, or even—"

"*Jared.*" He put more bite in his voice but then blasted a full-watt smile for the terrified job candidate. "What my brother's saying is that we'll be contacting you shortly if we need more information to move forward." Jaxson gestured her up from her seat.

The girl shot out of it like she was escaping prison.

"We're not done here," Jared said, his tone only half angry... the other half was bewildered as to why Jaxson was interrupting him.

"Oh yes, we are." Jaxson turned to Olivia. "Could you see our young friend out?" Her quick nod showed she was already completely clued-in to the Jared dynamic. Olivia put on a smile and gently on tugged the girl's elbow to usher her toward the front. Jaxson's gaze lingered a beat longer than necessary on Olivia's delicious rear-end and the way her skirt hugged her curves. He didn't know which turned him on more: the sway of her walk or the fact that she managed to get the freaked-out applicant to smile again before they disappeared around the corner.

Jaxson whipped back to his brother—he only had a few seconds before she returned. "How about if you don't terrify our new office assistant?"

"Terrify?" Jared pulled an almost comical expression of confusion. "Was she really scared?"

"Jared, she was shaking like a ninety-year-old man with palsy," Jaxson said, patiently, like he did every time his brother seemed oblivious to the people around him.

"Oh." Jared frowned, and this was the part that tore out Jaxson's heart. Because his brother had killed men from miles away with deadly sniper skills honed by both the Army and his own natural shifter talents… but he wouldn't hurt a fly otherwise. Not intentionally.

Jared still seemed confused. "I was just explaining—"

"Yeah, well, don't," Jaxson whispered quickly. Olivia's footsteps scuffed the carpet behind him, so he put on a smile and turned to her.

Olivia hooked a thumb over her shoulder. "I tried to tell her you guys were harmless. Kind of doubt she'll be back, though."

"That's all right." Jaxson turned to present her to Jared. "Olivia, this is my brother, Jared. He's generally in charge of operations, and we keep him far from the toner supply. Jared, meet Olivia Lilyfield, our new office assistant."

Jared's face opened in surprise, but only momentarily. Then it shut down like a bank vault closing. He rose, slowly. He was the largest of the three of them—and none of the River brothers were small—and he towered over Olivia.

She seemed undaunted, just smiling and sticking out her hand. "Pleasure to meet you, Jared."

Jared nodded and held her hand briefly, as if it were made of porcelain, and he might break it. Then he dropped his gaze to the floor and stared at his boots, still caked with mud from the Olympic mountains.

Jared nodded at his boots like he'd just now noticed them. "I better go get cleaned up." Then he lumbered away without another word.

Jaxson sucked in a slow breath and hoped his brother would actually go home and get a shower, not trek back to the mountains, dejected and depressed. Again.

The rest of the office was still pretty quiet—Jared must have worked the pack pretty hard to have so many MIA on a Monday. But at least that left Jaxson and Olivia alone.

Once Jared disappeared around the corner, Olivia said, "Yeah... he doesn't like me."

Jaxson shook his head. "It's not you, trust me. It's definitely him."

"Is that going to be a problem?" she asked, as if her employment might hinge on Jared and his moods. Her frown was substantial, like this really worried her. She *had* mentioned a rent payment was due.

Jaxson placed a hand on her shoulder. "Absolutely not. I'm the CEO around here, and if I say you're in, you're in." He could feel the heat of her skin through the thin fabric of her blouse, but not that tingly sensation from before. That must only come from skin-to-skin contact... he had to shove that thought away before his mouth started to water. But his wolf was rumbling happy growls again. Jaxson wondered what in the world he was thinking—she would be at the office every day. There was no way his willpower was going to hold out forever.

He gestured to the just-vacated seats. "While we have a moment alone, let's discuss the situation with finding a mate."

She slid into a chair and threw a glance around the office. "I'm assuming this topic is confidential?"

He took the seat opposite her. "Very much so." He waved a hand at the darkened offices. "If the pack knew I

JAXSON

was trying to delay choosing a mate, it would weaken my position as their alpha. Even my brothers would be dismayed."

Olivia frowned, but her dark, intelligent eyes were searching his face. "Jared seems like he might understand."

His eyebrows lifted. She was perceptive as well as smart. "Jared is the eldest. He could easily command the lead alpha position of our pack. He found his mate, but… well, let's just say he lost her."

Olivia's frown grew. "How does this mating thing work, exactly? I mean, I've heard that shifters mate for life, but that's really all I know."

"The mating itself is a magical bond that strengthens both the alpha and his mate." A familiar pain stabbed his chest—he'd known for a long time that this was the one thrill in life he would never experience, but it still hurt to think about. And not just him—his wolf was howling a long, mournful cry.

Jaxson took a breath and continued, "Technically, mating is a transfer of some of the alpha's magic to his mate's blood. The bond makes the resulting shifter pups strong and healthy. Full shifter powers. And, of course, the mating provides a solid family unit for the raising of those pups." Another howl. Jaxson tried to work the tension in his shoulders out by rolling his neck.

"That doesn't sound so bad." Her voice was very soft. Pained almost.

That lost sound hurt him even more. His hand was out, touching hers before he realized what he was doing. The electric feel of her soft skin against his jolted him enough to make him pull back. He couldn't figure out what that was about.

"Mating's far from bad," he pressed on. "It's great really. One of the better things about being a shifter. It's just that... I need to buy some time before I can make that commitment." Somehow lying to her about this, especially with her helping him, seemed wrong. But he couldn't risk telling her the truth—he'd only just met her, and it wasn't the kind of secret he could afford to let loose.

She was nodding, but thoughtfully. Thank heavens the lost look was gone from her eyes. "So you need a delay."

"Yes."

"And how many contenders are there?" she asked. "I mean, are there certain requirements your future mate has to meet?"

He smiled and leaned forward on the table. "Are you asking me what like in a woman?"

She actually blushed.

He couldn't help smiling wider in having caused that reaction.

JAXSON

"Let me guess," she said, ducking her head. "Gorgeous, smart, and with a talent for keeping secrets." She peeked up.

He met her gaze. "That's a great start." God, what was he doing, flirting with her? He coughed and wiped away his smile. "It would help if she were a daughter of one of the three packs we should be making an alliance with. The daughters are all full-blood shifters, so that's not an issue. But they're not all equally... well..."

"Hot?" She smirked, but he didn't like her knowing look—like she was judging him, and he was coming up *shallow*. He was even more surprised how much that bothered him.

"It's not just that," he said, a little defensively. "It's not even primarily that. It's more like... a connection. Some shifters think there's just one mate for every wolf. And maybe that's true. But I think it has to be something more than just magic that binds you together. There should be... something else."

"You want to find your soul mate." The sadness was back in her eyes again.

His shoulders dropped. "I suppose that sounds silly."

"No, not at all."

He hated the pain suddenly back in her eyes. "I just want to be sure I'm making the right choice," he said softly, trying to draw her out of whatever deep well she had dropped into.

She sucked in a breath and nodded. Some of the darkness lifted. "Okay. Three possible mates from other packs. *Advantage:* political alliances. *Disadvantage:* possibly not your soul mate. What if you chose *none-of-the-above?* What if we went wide in our search? I don't know, are there a lot of eligible female shifters in the greater Seattle area?"

He smiled—at the effort she was putting in and the fact that it seemed to distract her from the sadness. "Actually, there's not really an abundance of alternatives. Female wolves are much more rare than males—it has to do with infant survival rates and, well, other factors. Witches for one."

Olivia's eyes bugged out. "Witches?"

He frowned. "You know witches exist, right?"

"Um... yeah... a little. I mean, I've heard stories about that, too." She cleared her throat. "What does that have to do with female wolves being rare?"

"Witches hunt them." Jaxson scowled. "Mated female wolves especially—they have powerful magic. The witches cut out their hearts to obtain it."

"Really?" She looked stricken and a little disbelieving. "I mean... *God.* How could a person do that?"

Jaxson let his face go cold. "Witches aren't *people,* Olivia. Not the way you and I understand them. Witches are cold, power-hungry, and generally full of themselves enough to think the rest of us exist to serve their crazy-ass whims. If you meet one in a dark alley, don't play the hero. Run the other way. Fast." He knew all too well how quickly a witch could ruin your life.

The blood seemed to drain from Olivia's face, and Jaxson cursed himself internally. He was no better than Jared, scaring the crap out of a woman he hoped would stick around long enough to... well, until Jaxson would be forced out the door of Riverwise himself. Maybe then he could have someone in his life. Not a mate—he would never have that—but maybe he could have something less magical, but still beautiful. Maybe with a gorgeous, smart woman like Olivia, even if she wasn't a shifter. He'd long known that a human would be his only choice in the end. If his wolf would stand for it. He certainly seemed to lust after Olivia, so maybe... Jaxson reached out to touch her hand, trying to calm the quivers in it. Her skin was crazy soft, and the spark of touching her washed through him.

Maybe being with a human could have its own kind of magic.

"Don't worry about witches," he said, trying to keep his voice soothing. "We haven't had any encounters with them in forever—and I don't anticipate we will. I was just saying that's why there aren't as many female shifters around as you might expect."

She nodded, but slowly pulled her hand out from under his. Then she folded her arms across her chest, which only reminded him of how ample it was.

He forced his gaze up to meet hers.

"So," she said, "the three females from the three packs—those are your only real choices?"

"I'm sure there are other female shifters in the city. But if I snubbed all three of our potential allies... well, I'd better have an extremely good reason."

She gave a sharp nod of agreement and unfolded her arms again. "Okay. So here's what you do. You make an announcement that you're taking this mating business very seriously. Issue a press release, or whatever you do in wolfy shifter circles."

He cracked a grin. "Wolfy?"

She waved a hand at him. "Wolves. Big and bad. However you want to spin it."

He leaned across the table and snatched her waving hand out of the air. "But we *are* big and bad." *Damn*, she was drawing him in without even trying.

She blushed, and it took everything he had not to pull her in for a kiss, but then she gave him the devil eye. "Save it for the ladies you're trying to mate with."

"Ouch!" He dropped her hand and leaned back, but he had to bite his lip to contain his smile.

"Now, listen up," she said, full bossy mode. "I'm about to solve all your problems."

He managed to tame the smile a little. "Do tell."

She drilled into him with those big brown eyes. "You're taking this mating business seriously, so you're going to date *all the girls*. It's like The Bachelor, only for shifters. You're not doing this to be picky or choosy or anything obnoxious like that. You're doing this for the good of all the packs—to make sure you make the best match, for both you and your future mate. The problem is, of course, that this will take time."

"Lots of time." He was nodding in agreement now.

"Right. You have to be fair. Give each girl their turn. Three months exclusive dating for each one. And that's just for the first round. Then you eliminate one girl from contention and date the remaining two more seriously. Say, another three months. That's a year of dating altogether. By then, you should know if you're meant to be mates... or not."

"A year." It seemed impossibly long to put up this charade, and at the same time, far too little time left in his life as alpha of the River pack. But it would give him enough time to get some major operations underway—and get the pack headed in the right direction. Not to mention get his brothers ready to carry on the pack duties without him. "I can work with a year."

She smiled. "Great!"

"There's only one problem."

Her face clouded. "What's that?"

He winced as he saw the hole in the plan. "There's this idea among shifters that finding your mate is a love-at-first-sight kind of thing."

"Really?" Her nose scrunched up. "A little archaic, don't you think?"

"Not really," he admitted. "It has to do with your inner wolves knowing when they meet their mates. There's an instant attraction. Something powerful, almost undeniable sometimes. It's part of the magic."

She frowned. "And you've already met these girls?"

"Oh yeah." He sighed. "Our packs have been working together for a while."

"And no instant sparks? No choirs of angels opening up the heavens?" She gestured wide with her hands.

He shook his head.

"No wonder you don't want to rush into this mating thing." She nodded like it was all becoming clear to her. But then she waved that away. "Doesn't matter. We'll just put it in the statement that your wolf is equally smitten with all three—that's why you're taking the unusual *human* step of actually dating the women you're going to potentially marry, er, mate with."

His eyebrows lifted again. "Actually, that's kind of

brilliant."

"Kind of?" she scoffed. "It's a wonder you guys got along without me here for so long."

He smiled wide. "Truly."

"Okay, you need to get started right away." She twirled her fingers at him. "Get me set up with a desk. I'll need a computer, names, and contact information. Before you know it, I'll have a dating schedule set up and a statement for you to give."

He rose up from his seat. "Yes, Ma'am." He smiled all the way to his office.

A year. A year to keep the mating pressures at bay, from both the other packs and his own. Twelve months to get some key operations under way and lay plans for the future of Riverwise without him. And three-hundred-and-sixty-five days of having Olivia Lilyfield in his office with her soft skin and sharp mind.

This was going to work out even better than he thought.

Chapter 5

Jaxson stared into the eyes of the red-haired beauty across the table from him.

Her name was Morrigan, she was the daughter of the alpha of the Northern pack, and she had an MBA from Northwestern and a body to die for. Only she really *would* die if Jaxson claimed her for his mate. But she didn't know that—*couldn't* know that—and with the sizzling hot looks she was sending over the oyster appetizers, he was pretty sure she was picturing them in bed at this exact moment. Her eyes were half-lidded and kept roaming his body. She was probably imagining the best orgasm of her

JAXSON

life—which was no doubt what a *normal* mating would be.

Jaxson sighed and waved over the waiter. "Another please." He held up his club soda.

"Of course, sir." The tuxedoed waiter slipped away.

"Wouldn't you like something a little stronger?" Morrigan asked, raising her glass of red wine.

"Have to work tomorrow." He gestured to the crimson liquid. "How's your Merlot?"

"Delicious." She took a long, luxurious sip, probably thinking it was sexy—all it did was remind Jaxson he'd rather be somewhere else. Anywhere else.

The Café Mer had a glittering view of the bay and was one of the fanciest restaurants in Seattle—the perfect first-date spot for someone serious about finding a mate. At least, that's what Olivia said when she made the reservation two days ago. Riverwise's clients frequented places like this, but Jaxson didn't have much use for the extravagance. However, Olivia was determined to make the ruse convincing, and he had to agree the setting was beautiful—brass fixtures, polished wooden floors, artistic lighting that complemented the cityscape below.

There just wasn't any magic in the conversation. Or the company.

"So your MBA must come in handy at the office," Jaxson tried. Even his small talk was coming out miniscule.

"Northern Peaks is a *law firm*," Morrigan said with a smirk. "They tend to think of an MBA as that thing you get when you can't quite make it into law school."

"Oh." He cringed. "Sorry, I—"

"Jaxson, I'm *teasing*." Her green eyes widened a little like she couldn't believe how dense he was.

Great. He was completely off his game tonight. "Right. I completely knew that." He tried for a sheepish smile, but it just felt empty.

Olivia had spent a full half hour before the date admonishing him to look past his prejudices and prior experience to give the date—and Morrigan—a chance. His delicious office assistant seemed determined to find him a soul mate before the one-year expiration of this ruse, and he had promised her he would try. But *trying* couldn't create a magical spark that didn't exist. And while Morrigan was undeniably beautiful—with the smoldering sexiness of an alpha female shifter—she just didn't float his boat. Riverwise had worked with Northern Peaks on a few cases when his clients needed some very discreet legal opinions, but the entire pack was... *stiff*. It was the only word he could come up with, and he supposed it made sense for a pack comprised of lawyers and MBAs, but it didn't help him pretend to find his date fascinating.

His wolf was off sulking in a corner.

JAXSON

Jaxson sighed and gazed out at the twinkling lights of the bay.

What was Olivia doing right now? Was she at the library, looking for whatever her true dream job was? The gig at Riverwise had to be temporary in her mind. Something to pay the bills. She would tolerate it until she could move on to something better. Would she even last the whole year? Maybe she was waiting by her phone for him to call with an update—

"Jaxson."

His attention snapped away from the thousand-mile-gaze out across the bay and back to the female shifter who was his date. Her claws were about to come out, with the way her face was flushed and her eyes were boring into him. She must have said something he missed.

Jaxson put on his contrite face. "I'm so sorry, Morrigan. I'm distracted tonight, and that's really not fair to you."

Her hiked-up shoulders relaxed. "Is everything all right?"

He breathed out another sigh. It felt like he'd had a hundred sighs already on this date. "Just work. Nothing I can discuss, unfortunately." That much was true.

She nodded, and her eyes lit up again. "There must be all kinds of exciting things you can't share in the security business." A small smile snuck on her face.

"We're actually in the business of keeping things *unexciting*—our clients pay us to keep the fireworks far away from their personal lives. Which we usually manage to do. But if something goes down, we debrief it, break it down, discuss it internally. Everything stays within the pack. You know how it is."

"What about your mate? Will she be privy to all the juicy celebrity secrets?" Morrigan arched her eyebrows and took another sip of her wine.

He forced a smile on to his face. "Of course. Although I can think of more interesting things to talk about in bed." He tried for a flirtatious lift of his eyebrow, but it all felt *off*. He hadn't thought of a mate as a potential security leak, but now…

She leaned forward, lacing her fingers. "What sorts of interesting things?" He didn't know if she was deliberately thrusting her breasts forward, but they strained against the low-cut, sleeveless black dress that was trying to contain them.

He lingered his gaze there, which she obviously wanted—Olivia should be proud of how hard he was trying here—but there was really no point to it. The last thing he wanted was to actually *feel* something for Morrigan. It would be just that much harder when the ruse was revealed. And when he left his pack altogether.

JAXSON

Jaxson dragged his gaze up to Morrigan's face. Her lips were parted, and it wasn't hard to scent the arousal on her. "Things that wouldn't be polite to say in a crowded public restaurant."

"I guess we'll have to save that for later this evening."

He wouldn't be taking her home, so there was no point in letting that hang in the air. And clearly she was angling for some kind of first-date advantage in this *Dating Game* that Olivia had invented. The idea that Morrigan was actually *competing* for this chance at being his mate... just chilled the entire thing for him.

"So tell me about your role at Northern Peaks," he said, deliberately cooling his tone.

She leaned back, disappointed.

He couldn't help sneaking a look at his phone. He was just checking the time, he told himself. But he also noticed there were no messages from Olivia.

Olivia stared at the mess of files on her computer. She'd only been at Riverwise for two days; she couldn't undo months of disastrous accounting in that short amount of time. She knew that, but it was still frustrating. Just deciphering the complex filing system that Jared River used to store receipts for office expenses was like figuring out the Rosetta stone with only two languages.

And the reimbursements for the other pack members? Filed completely at random as far as she could tell. Half were scanned and stuffed into electronic folders, while the other half filled a cardboard legal box. And some were duplicates, which just made everything worse.

Olivia sighed. It was late, and her eyes were starting to cross. She should go home and start over in the morning. She needed a fresh mind to tackle the mountainous task of organizing Riverwise's business into something halfway logical. But she knew exactly why she had stayed at the office way past when the rest of the pack had left—Jaxson River was on a date with a hot redhead, and that image would just fester in her mind if she went home to her empty apartment. There was nothing to distract her there, not the way a thousand misfiled receipts in the office could do.

So she buried herself in paperwork and tried not to think about her gorgeous shifter boss bringing home a hot female wolf to see if they had "chemistry." Or maybe gazing deep into her eyes and finding his soul mate there.

Olivia groaned. Who was she kidding? Even the office accounting mess couldn't keep her focused. She ran her hands over her face, rubbed the blurriness from her eyes, then clicked through to the folder she'd put together on the three female shifters Jaxson would be dating.

For a year.

JAXSON

She didn't know why that bothered her so much—it was literally *her job* to find him a mate. And she wholeheartedly wanted him to find happiness; there was way too much sadness in those gorgeous blue eyes. But there was a small, selfish part of her that simply squirmed at the thought of him putting his hands on another woman.

As if he would ever put his hands on her.

She was plump, only moderately attractive, and most importantly... *not a wolf.* Even if Jaxson, for some reason, missed all those rather important details, there could never be anything more than a hot kiss in an alleyway between them. Because she was half-witch, and eventually that would come out. Jaxson's work was high-end cyber security, for god's sake. He would find out what happened to her parents if he bothered to look. And he was too smart not to look.

Olivia sighed and clicked open the file for Morrigan North, the female shifter from the Northern pack. Of the three contenders, Olivia liked her the least. She was all wrong for Jaxson, at least on paper. Her MBA project was a long dissertation on how to pull companies out of bankruptcy and reorganize them for maximum efficiency. Olivia supposed it was useful for a law firm like Northern Peaks, but it sounded like dry legal wrangling to her. And quasi-sleazy business speak as well.

The second candidate wasn't much better—Thea from the Blue Mountain pack was a brown-haired accountant and the least attractive of the three. Although, to be honest, all three were ridiculously good looking. Must be the shifter gene—Olivia noticed every shifter in the office, which was the vast majority of employees at Riverwise, was supernaturally hot. She'd spent the entire first day staring at her feet in order not to gape at the bulging biceps and powerfully-built rear-ends of the Riverwise staff. The women were gorgeous, too, but only a couple of them were shifters. Jaxson was right about female wolves being relatively rare, at least in the office.

Which made it all the more unusual for three female shifters to be competing to be Jaxson's mate. But that didn't surprise her at all—he was brilliant and funny and panty-meltingly hot. His time in the SEALs only made him more swoon-worthy. And he was a natural alpha—commander for his unit in the Navy and now CEO of Riverwise as a civilian. Olivia had created a file on him in the course of her match-making, and it just highlighted how much Jaxson had to offer a mate. A mate who would definitely not be *her*. In spite of that obvious fact, she couldn't help wanting him every time he stepped into her office. It wasn't her fault—he was all alpha, with a natural ease that would be irresistible to any female. And she'd grown to simply *like* him as well. He was funny and kind and...

Olivia sighed. She *had* to stop crushing on her boss. She flipped through the files again.

The third shifter hoping to become Mrs. Jaxson River was the one Olivia both admired the most and feared would be *The One* for Jaxson. Terra was a raven-haired beauty with soulful dark eyes. An artist with a wild streak, she spent most of her teens roaming the streets of Seattle and taking pictures of the homeless or other denizens of the street. She had just turned twenty-one, and she was already one of the city's up-and-coming artists, with three gallery exhibitions this year alone. And her pictures were *good*. Olivia had checked them out online, and they somehow brought out the bright inner light of even the darkest, dingiest corners of the city.

Terra's pack was different—a collection of shifters tied together by bloodlines but not in business with each other. The Wilding pack had a research professor at the university, an entrepreneurial inventor with his own company, and even a colonel in the Army among their scattered count. Their pack operations were looser, with each individual striking out independently to make their marks upon the world.

That sounded more like Jaxson. And Olivia was certain, once he had a chance to spend time with the beautiful and passionate shifter girl-artist, he would find the mate he was looking for.

Then he'd likely never look at Olivia again.

She covered her face with her hands and leaned back in the black leather chair of her new office. She really had to stop thinking about him that way. One hot kiss in an alleyway didn't mean anything. Which didn't stop her from playing it over and over in her mind… another thing she *really* needed to stop doing. But that only brought the heat back to her face—

"That bad, is it?" a deep voice said from the doorway.

It jolted her and made her chair squeak. Her hands flew away from her face, and her mouth fell open. Jaxson stood in the doorway, leaning against the doorjamb with his arms crossed, a smirk on his face and a laugh dancing in his brilliant blue eyes. His white silk shirt—the one she had helped pick out for his date—was just thin enough to cling attractively to the strong muscles of his arms where he'd rolled up the sleeves.

"What are you doing here?" was all she managed to get out. She glanced at the screen. "It's only nine o'clock."

Jaxson unlocked his arms, strode over to her desk, and leaned against it, stretching out his long legs. They almost brushed against hers dangling off the edge of her chair. "The date was a bust."

"Already?" But her heart wasn't unhappy about that,

JAXSON

not really.

Jaxson shook his head and glanced at the screen. She had left the image files open with pictures of the three candidates. A flush of embarrassment swept across Olivia's face, but Jaxson just sighed when he turned back to her.

"I don't know if I can keep this up for a year."

"Wow, that painful, huh?" Olivia bit her lip. Maybe she shouldn't have lined up the least likely of the candidates first.

Jaxson's gaze dropped to her lips, so she untucked them. Then he frowned and pierced her with a hard look. "You *knew* it would go badly, didn't you?"

She tried not to cringe, but she was sure the guilt was printed across her forehead in forty-eight point font. "I didn't *know*... but I kind of suspected."

He wagged his finger at her. "You worked overtime to convince me to give her a chance."

Olivia held up her hands. "Well, *did you?* I mean, really? There's only so much I can do here with elegant restaurants and candle-lit dinners."

"There were no candles." He scowled. "And I'd rather take a knife to the chest than sit through another dinner with Morrigan North. Less pain, and at least the scars would be visible."

"*Jaxson.*" She gave him an exaggerated look of

impatience. "You're never going to find a mate with that attitude."

He frowned and dropped his gaze to study his polished black shoes. The worry lines were back on his face again, and it twisted her stomach. It was like the creases in his forehead were fissures in his soul, weathered and worn, but only she could see them. It propelled her up from her chair, and she was standing in front of him before she knew what she planned to do.

"Hey," she said, teetering because she was suddenly too close to him but couldn't really back away without making it *more* awkward. "Don't listen to me. I don't know what I'm saying. I'm the last person to know anything about mates or even dating, really. You should probably fire me as a dating consultant. I'm much better at filing, though, I promise."

He smiled, but some of that sadness he carried inside leaked out and poisoned it. "But it's true. I'm never going to have a mate." His voice had turned soft.

"Don't say that." She dropped her voice, whispering now, like him. "There's someone out there who's *The One*, and you *deserve* to find her. Besides, we're just getting started. I'm not giving up, so you're not allowed to, either. I may be the world's worst dating consultant, but I'm going to find you that soul mate, if it's the last thing I do." And at that moment, she meant every word. She couldn't stand the lost look on his face.

He stood up from leaning against the desk—which didn't help with the *standing too close* part—but he smiled a little more, and it lifted her heart. "You're a very stubborn woman."

"You have no idea, Jaxson River. So don't tell me—" Her words were cut off when he raised his hand to touch his fingertips to her cheek. *What was he doing?* His gaze dropped to her lips, so she shut her gaping mouth. She had no air to form words, anyway.

"You know..." He leaned closer, his voice a husky whisper. "It so happens that I'm between dates at the moment."

"You have a date with Thea on Saturday," she breathed, but she couldn't bring herself to pull away. Her heart thumped so loudly, she wondered if he could hear it.

"I'm a free man for two days, then." He drew closer and slipped a hand behind her back. What was he doing? Was he really going to kiss her?

"You're... you're supposed to be..." She tried to protest, but she didn't want to, not really. And his nearness, his electric touch on her skin, was scrambling her brain.

"I'm big and bad, remember?" he whispered as his lips brushed her cheek. "I don't do what I'm supposed to."

The last words crashed against her lips along with his mouth. His arms encased her body in a steel cage of muscle, but the last thing she wanted was to escape. The shock of his hungry lips on hers made her forget to kiss him back—but her body responded instinctively. She melted into his chest, her hands clawed at his back, and her mouth opened to him. He plunged his tongue inside, and by the time she tried to return the kiss—to counter the total domination of her mouth by his—he just groaned, twirled her around, and pushed her rear-end against the desk, trapping her between his rock hard body and the unforgiving wood of the desk. She was consumed by his lips, and she didn't think the kiss could get any hotter, but then his hands started mapping her body. His fingers trailed hot lines of fire down her arms, around the small of her waist, and up her back. She gasped when he brushed the side of her breast, then rounded the palm of his hand against it, lifting and squeezing it and moaning against her mouth.

The heat was gushing between her legs, and every part of her body was fully alive under his commanding touch. She could barely breathe, and she had *no idea* what he was thinking, but his touch and his strength and his overwhelming masculine *need* for her was destroying any attempt at rational thought.

His mouth broke from hers, allowing her to gasp in

JAXSON

air, but his urgent nips at her neck made her head tip back and her eyes roll up. *Oh God, it's been so long...* and no man had *ever* touched her the way Jaxson River was right now.

His hand slipped under her shirt, where his fingers played electric fire on her skin. "Olivia." He was panting against her neck. "Why do you taste so good?" The tip of his tongue flicked across her skin. "I want to touch every part of you."

His words clenched the muscles tight and low in her belly. His fingers slipped inside her bra. Her breasts were large, but his hands were more than big enough to cup them. When his fingers found her rapidly hardening nipples, he growled a low sound, deep in his throat.

Yes. She dug her short nails even deeper into his back, feeling his muscles tense and flex through the thin fabric of his shirt. None of this made any sense. There was no reason for Jaxson River to want her like this—her of all people—but she wasn't going to stop him. Even if it was just a quick tryst on her desk. She ached for every touch and panted whisper he would give her.

Footsteps sounded outside her office, followed by a rushed voice, saying, "Olivia, do you know where—"

The words cut off as whoever it was reached the door and swung to a stop inside. Olivia's whole body jerked with the shock of being caught, and Jaxson suddenly stilled in his fervent explorations of her body. They both turned at once to look at the door.

Jaxson's brother Jace stood there, slack-jawed, but with a slightly horrified look on his face. Olivia's face flamed, but it was made worse by the way Jaxson shoved away from her so fast it was almost like he magically transported a foot away.

He was embarrassed. Caught making out with a human when he's supposed to be looking for a female shifter mate.

Olivia wanted to sink into the floor.

Chapter 6

A vacuum of embarrassment killed all sound in the room.

Olivia couldn't decide if she should make some excuse for why Jaxson had her trapped against her desk with his hand up her shirt... or if she should just leave it to him. She had no explanation whatsoever for it anyway. Jaxson said nothing, silently adjusting his shirt and glaring at his brother, who was still standing in the doorway.

"Um," Jace said, obviously also struggling for words. "Sorry to interrupt your... *work*..." He hesitated again, looking more perplexed than disapproving. Then he shook his head and swung a serious look to Jaxson. "We have a problem."

"What is it?" Jaxson's voice was flat and calm, completely in charge, as if he hadn't just been caught making out.

For some reason, this flushed even more embarrassment through Olivia. She knew she was just some quick fling for him, but being thrust aside so obviously was… well, humiliating. She swallowed down the angry words that wanted to pop out and pretended to shuffle some papers on her desk. What was she doing, making out with her boss, anyway? Any fool knew that never worked out. Especially given the situation. She was impossibly stupid for even—

"Cassie Wilding is missing." Jace's voice cut through her barrage of thoughts.

Olivia looked up. "Wilding? Like the Wilding wolf pack?" She frowned and scoured her memory. She'd been focused on eligible mates for Jaxson, but the name *did* sound familiar.

Jace frowned at her, then strode the rest of the way into the room and dropped his voice when he reached his brother. "Maybe we should discuss this in private?" he asked quietly. He obviously meant Olivia.

She dropped her gaze to the floor. "I'll just… see myself out." She fumbled to grab her phone and wallet out of the drawer.

Jaxson took two quick steps to her side and stopped her with his hand on hers. She dragged her gaze up to meet his.

"This is a pack matter." There was an apology on his face that he wasn't speaking out loud. "But I'd like you to stay. You're part of Riverwise now—you should know what's going on."

A pack matter. The politics between the packs had a heavy influence on Jaxson's ideas of who to pick for a mate. That was the real reason why he wanted her to stay.

She nodded, short and fast, to show she understood. "I know how to keep my mouth shut."

He gave her a small, approving smirk before turning back to his brother. "I'll read Olivia in on this afterward, but first—what's happened to Cassie?"

Jace had a deep frown for the whole interaction, but he quickly explained. "She was taken off the street. A white van just pulled up, and two men snatched her outside her school. She was staying late at some private academy the Wilding's send their pups to—"

"Wait," Olivia interrupted. "Pups? Is she a kid?" It was quickly coming back to her—there was a whole litter of young wolves in the Wilding pack.

Jaxson nodded to her. "Cassie is Terra Wilding's younger sister. She's about twelve." He swung back to

Jace. "How long ago?"

"Less than an hour."

Jaxson scowled. "So you think she's at the shelter."

"She might be," Jace said. "If we get there fast enough, we might be able to stop them…"

"…before they transport her away," Jaxson finished.

"Exactly." Jace grimaced in the direction of the doorway. Precious seconds were ticking away. "Jared's back up in the mountains."

"Dammit." Jaxson curled up his fist and pressed it to his mouth for a moment. "All right, we'll have to move without him." His voice was back in full command mode. "We take whoever in the pack you can get hold of in the next five minutes. Then we move out. Time is against us."

Jace nodded, already whipping his phone out of his pocket. "I'll meet you downstairs in five. We'll need supplies, too."

"On it." Jaxson turned to take Olivia by the shoulders as Jace raced from the room. "I'm sorry to drag you into this. But the Wildings may call while we're out, and I need someone here to hold down the fort. Keep them calm. And reassure them we're doing everything we can."

She nodded quickly. "Fort-holding, phone-answering, and re-assuring. I can handle that. Only… what do I tell them? And shouldn't we be calling the police or something?"

Jaxson took a deep breath and let out a slow, angry sigh. "The police aren't much help to shifters, Olivia. I know that might not make any sense, but they figure it's all turf wars and pack fights. And they stay out. Plus, once they know we're shifters…"

"Oh. Right." She knew about the laws regarding shifter registration. Once someone was a known shifter, they had to submit DNA samples in both shifter and human forms, in case they ever committed a crime. That way the police could tie them to the crime, even if they did it in shifter form. She'd never thought about it before, but it was pretty ridiculous to treat shifters that way—like they were sub-humans who were already criminals. But then she'd never kissed one before and realized just how *human* a shifter could be.

"The other packs already know most of the situation," Jaxson continued. "We've been in talks about how to handle it with them, so I might as well brief you now on it now, so you're not caught off guard." His face was grim. "Shifters have been disappearing for a while."

"Disappearing?" She frowned. "You mean going missing?"

He nodded. "At first, it was just lone wolves vanishing off the streets. Then a few from the smaller shifter gangs downtown went missing. Being in the security business,

Riverwise hears things. For a while, it seemed random. Maybe some rogue witch at work, harvesting shifters for her Dark Arts."

Olivia cringed. "But now you think it's more than that?"

"It's definitely more," he said. "The pace has been picking up, plus we've begun to see some of the first wolves who disappeared show up again. And they're pretty messed up. Sick. A couple have died since their release."

"Release?" she asked, her face scrunching up in revulsion. "From where? Who's doing this?"

"That's what I was trying to find out when you interrupted me in the alleyway."

She thought about the men, the ones using the cattle prods on Jaxson, and her stomach curled into one giant knot.

Jaxson gave a soft smile at her distressed look. "It's all right. You were trying to do the right thing. I can't fault you for that." He traced a finger along her cheek that just stirred up feelings she really shouldn't have for this incredibly brave and sexy man. But her lips were still swollen from his kiss devouring her only a minute ago. That didn't exactly help.

She brushed all that aside. "I had a feeling something was wrong with that shelter. So you think whoever took

Cassie might be taking her there?"

"The shelter's a way-station of some kind," Jaxson said. "The shifters were released near there. And some of the ones who disappeared might have processed through there at one point. If we move fast and if we're lucky, we'll find Cassie there before they move her on to wherever they're holding the missing wolves. If we don't find her there, I'm going to locate someone inside that place who knows what's going on and persuade him to tell us where they've taken her."

"Persuade." She swallowed—she could easily picture Jaxson in his hulking, snarling wolf form. She wouldn't mess with him, but these people… they might have guns. Then again, Jaxson was an ex-SEAL. They probably had more to fear from him than the other way around—no matter what form he was in. But she couldn't help worrying. "That sounds… dangerous."

The muscles in Jaxson's cheek worked silently for a moment. "It takes a lot to kill a shifter, Olivia. And yet these people have practically destroyed full-grown gang members three times Cassie's size. I'm not going to let them play with a twelve-year-old girl."

She nodded quickly. Of course not. Because that's the kind of man Jaxson was. She blinked back tears and impulsively threw her arms around his neck. "Go get the bastards," she whispered, then pulled back just as quickly, nervous that it had been too much.

A crooked smile hung on Jaxson's face for a moment, then he slipped one hand behind her head and pulled her in for a fierce and fast kiss. Before she could react, he was gone, hurrying out her office door after his brother. Off to save the little sister of a beautiful shifter female who would no doubt claim his heart when it was all done. Olivia could see it unfolding now… because if there was one thing she was certain of, it was that Jaxson River would rescue that little girl. Or die trying.

And Terra Wilding, his perfect mate, would be eternally grateful.

CHAPTER 7

Jaxson held up two fingers to signal Jace to hold his position.

His brother echoed the command to the three members of the River pack behind him. They held still in the shadows of the alleyway next to the homeless shelter. Their clothes weren't exactly suited for their mission—Murphy, Taylor, and Rich were still in their business casual from the office, Jace wore his usual jeans and grungy band t-shirt, and Jaxson still had on his silk shirt and dress pants from the disaster date. But they'd picked up enough guns, blades, and tech to fight their way through most situations… including breaking into a homeless shelter to rescue a shifter kid.

Only there would be more than warm soup waiting for them inside.

Jaxson edged to the front of the shelter. A light was on over the main door, but it was closed. There was no activity out front.

"All clear," Jaxson said, low enough that his voice wouldn't carry. "Let's take the door in back."

If they were in wolf form, they could communicate with their thoughts, but they were in the middle of the city, and even at nine-thirty on a Friday in this part of town, a pack of wolves roaming the streets would be noticed. There were no unmarked vans or other suspicious vehicles in back. Jaxson had parked a block away in order to approach on foot and catch whoever had Cassie by surprise.

He had his suspicions about who might be running this snatch-and-release program with shifters. The first possibility was the local Seattle PD, deciding to rough up some shifters to send a message to the gangs. But that didn't make sense with the sick shifters that had been released. Shifters healed quickly unless you messed with the magic in their blood—that meant someone was tormenting shifters in a more substantial, long-lasting, and intentional way. Which spelled *government operation* to him. Either that or some sadistic bastard with a grudge against shifters who could afford to commandeer a homeless shelter. No, it had to be government-sanctioned—the only question was whether it was military or intelligence-based.

In the SEALs, he commanded an elite corps of men who used every ability—including their shifter skills—to take down the enemy whenever and wherever their CO sent them. Jaxson trusted his brothers-in-arms as much as his own pack, who were literally bound to him with their magical oath. But he'd seen enough unstable personalities sneak past the psych evals. Or go bad on re-integration, casualties of the battlefield, only with scars you couldn't see. He understood that—his own brothers brought that lesson home to him. But the scale of this operation was more than one rogue military washout.

This was something put in motion by someone in power.

Which made his blood run cold.

Jaxson hugged the wall next to the back door. The others lined up beside him, close, ready to hustle inside once the door was sprung. He tested the door, quietly—locked. He waved over Taylor, who already had his electronic lockpick ready to go. He crouch-ran up to the door, tapped through the sequence, and they all held their breaths as the box cycled through the combinations.

The door clicked open.

They crept down a short hallway with storage rooms on either side. At the end, Jaxson held up a fist to signal the pack to stop. He listened—chatter came from down the hall to the right. Conversational and muffled, like through a closed door. On silent feet, they turned the corner and found the one back office room spilling light out from under the door. And laughter.

Jaxson edged closer and very slowly tested the doorknob—it turned minutely. He held up three fingers, made eye contact with his men, then counted down...three...two...one...

He whipped open the door. Murphy and Taylor led the way, storming the room with shouts and drawn weapons. Jace and Rich were right behind them. Jaxson swept the hallway, covering their backs and arriving last in the room, only to find it already secure.

Murphy stood over one beefy guy in overalls, but the man was knocked out. Jaxson shook his head, and Murphy winced an apology. They couldn't get intel from the unconscious. Fortunately, Jace was holding back his blade from slicing the second man's throat... although he looked like he wanted to. Badly.

In addition to the blade against his throat, the dark-haired man was being held by Taylor and Rich. Their prisoner looked like his face had been rearranged by

JAXSON

more than one thug-fight. His stance was calm, body still, not resisting, no visible signs of fear. The man was almost certainly ex-military, possibly contractor ops—either that or the homeless shelter was hiring some serious badass employees.

Jaxson waved Murphy toward the door. "Sweep the center." But he didn't expect they'd find Cassie. If she was here, she would have been locked in with these two goons.

"Where's the girl?" Jaxson asked Thug Life, not bothering with preamble.

He smirked but otherwise didn't move. "I don't know what you're talking about."

Jaxson nodded and slowly walked up to the man. He was big, almost as tall as Jaxson, but even big men had something they feared. Not always pain, although enough of that could be persuasive. Something more primal was often more effective.

Jaxson lifted his chin to Jace, who eased off on the blade. Jaxson held up his hand, palm out, in front of the man's face.

In a calm voice, he said, "Here's how this is going to go." He glanced at his hand and commanded it to shift, slowly growing five razor-sharp claws. They inched toward the man's face as they grew. He leaned back, but his calm expression had evaporated. For non-shifters, the idea of being taken apart by claws and teeth often struck more fear than a blade or bullet. It wasn't the pain so much as the horror of it. It conjured fears of being eaten alive, and the primal part of the brain—the part that had evolved a million years ago when man's enemies had claws and fangs—had an instinctual fear of it built in.

"You're going to tell me where the girl is," Jaxson said quietly. "And you're going to tell me now. Or I'm going to claw and bite the answer out of you, one chunk at a time."

The man paled and blinked rapidly.

Jaxson might have to draw some blood, but it shouldn't have to go much further than that. Only enough to convince the man that Jaxson was serious. And he was. Very serious.

Cassie didn't have time for him to mess around.

Chapter 8

Olivia would end up wearing a hole in Riverwise's carpet with the way she was pacing her office. But she had to stay near the phone in case Jaxson called. Or someone from the Wilding pack. Or the hospital, saying that there had been a horrible tragedy at the homeless shelter and could she please come identify the bodies? Olivia sucked in a deep breath, dragged her hands across her face, and slapped her cheeks a couple times to stop that line of thought.

They're going to be fine.

She snuck another peek at the local news on her

phone, just to see if there was anything about a kidnapping or a shifter fight breaking out downtown. Nothing. Of course.

She slumped into her chair, thinking maybe she should try to do some work to distract herself, when a buzzing sound floated in from the front. Only when it was followed up with some banging did she realize it was someone at the door. She sprinted through the office to the frosted-glass entrance. She had to bang around with the lock a few times before she could spring it loose.

A gorgeous dark-haired woman brushed past her on the way in. "Where's Jaxson?" she demanded but didn't wait for an answer. She just strode around the corner toward the offices in back. A man hurried in after her. He was tall, well-built, broad-shouldered... and dark-haired gorgeous as well. He hardly slowed down and ignored Olivia just like the woman.

"Terra," he called after her, his voice annoyed. Then he disappeared around the corner, too.

Olivia closed the door and followed after them, but obviously they were both shifters from the Wilding pack. When she reached the conference room, Terra was muttering something—half curses, half mumbled arguments—but her claws were out and slashing the air as she raced along the offices, looking in each one.

"Where is he, where is he..."

JAXSON

At least, that's what Olivia thought she was saying.

Then Terra reached the last office. Not finding whatever she was looking for, she turned toward Olivia and screeched. *"Where is he?"*

"Terra, calm down." The man had reached her and tried to take her by the shoulders, but she just shoved him aside. Olivia gasped as Terra's claws sliced across the man's chest, shredding his shirt and causing a bloom of blood to darken it.

"Goddamn it, Terra!" he said, but he just followed after her as she took off again.

That's when Olivia noticed Terra was heading straight toward her like a black-haired thunderstorm, eyes blazing with lightning. Olivia's heart lurched, but she held her ground. She didn't even bother putting up her hands in defense against Terra's claws. Probably just get them sliced anyway.

When Terra arrived in front of her, all sound and fury, Olivia said quietly, "I know you're worried about Cassie."

Terra came to a teetering halt in front of her, and the storm in her eyes melted tears from the corners. "Do you know where she is?"

"Not yet." Olivia was proud of how calm her voice was compared to her pounding heart. "But Jaxson will bring her home. You can count on that."

Terra let out a breath, like it was escaping her without

her volition. "How do you know?"

"Because he said he would." Her words held all the conviction she felt in her heart. Even if she'd only known the man for a few days, she knew he kept his word. In fact, she'd known that much from the first few minutes, when he promised not to hurt her, and she believed him enough to give the electric prod over to him.

"Jaxson's taken four of his pack members and gone after your sister," Olivia continued. "The minute he finds her, he'll call and let you know. He said you might be coming here."

Terra was nodding, over and over in a distracted way, but Olivia's words seemed to be having a calming effect.

Olivia reached out a tentative hand to lightly pat Terra's arm—staying clear of the still-flexing claws. "I'm sorry I don't have more news for you yet."

Terra stared at Olivia's hand, so she pulled it back. But the female shifter's face wasn't horrified... just confused. She looked up. "Who *are* you?"

"Oh... um..." Olivia folded her arms across her chest. "Just the secretary."

The man accompanying Terra had been hanging back, but now he edged forward and laid a gentle hand on Terra's shoulder. He arched an eyebrow at Olivia. "Sounds like Riverwise has made a recent and very smart hiring move."

He lifted his hand from Terra's shoulder and extended it to Olivia. "My name's Trent Wilding. I'm the crazy girl's younger brother." His hand was warm, and his smile kind.

"Olivia Lilyfield." He didn't seem bothered by the red stains across his chest, but she had to ask anyway… "Are you all right? I mean, I've heard shifters heal fast, but I could get the first-aid kit, if you would like."

Trent broke out into a wide grin. "You *are* new, aren't you?"

Olivia blushed and ducked her head, feeling like a fool.

"It would be nice if everyone was as considerate as Ms. Lilyfield here," Trent said. Those words were directed at Terra, but they made Olivia feel better enough to peek up at him. He smiled with enough flirtation to make her blush again.

"Can I get you two something to drink?" Olivia asked, trying to move on. "I can fire up the coffee pot. You're welcome to stay as long as you'd like. I mean, until we hear news."

Terra didn't answer, just drifted over to one of the couches in the center of the room. Trent watched her go with a pinched look. As Terra perched on the edge of the couch, tears slid down her cheeks, flowing freely one after another. She was staring into space and twisting her hands.

Trent's warm hand landed on Olivia's shoulder and interrupted her staring. "How about I help you with that coffee?" His long-lashed, black eyes were sparkling, but he didn't seem in tears over his younger sister the way Terra was.

Olivia nodded and ushered him back to the lunch room. It was small—even the whole pack couldn't fit in there at once—and it was just a converted office, but it had a coffee maker on the counter by the sink. Olivia filled the pot with water. The gushing sound of the tap muted any conversation for a moment, but Olivia was painfully aware of how Trent was checking her out. Not like he thought she was hot—more like she was a zoo specimen that fascinated him.

Once she poured the water into the coffeemaker, the silence became more obvious. "Is your sister going to be all right? Terra, I mean." She only flicked a look at Trent, who was leaned against the counter, watching her measure out coffee.

"Terra is overly dramatic in the calmest of situations." He sighed. "But she's very close to Cassie. Our mother died when Cassie was still a baby, so she's really more a daughter than a sister. Although Terra's really no one's idea of a mother." There was a teasing laugh in his voice, but also an incredible amount of love for both his sisters.

JAXSON

Olivia could hear it.

She finished setting up the pot and flipped the switch to run. "I know how hard it is to lose a parent when you're young." She pursed her lips and peered at Trent.

He was still studying her, but a frown had gathered on his forehead. "Do you? I'm sorry."

She shook her head. "It was a long time ago."

His face opened in curiosity. "But you still carry the scars."

That made her heart stutter. Was it that obvious? "I just..." But there was no way she could explain that she didn't just *lose* them, like you lose your keys. And they weren't *stolen* from her, the way Cassie had been taken. She was responsible for their deaths. And that was a wound that would never heal. *Shouldn't* heal. "I'm just saying, I'm glad you and your sisters had each other. And I'm sure Jaxson will bring Cassie back to you. He's a good man."

Trent shifted a little closer, still eyeing her curiously. "Yet he's not a man. He's a wolf. A wolf who's hired a human as a secretary."

Her back stiffened. "I don't need to be a wolf to run the accounting."

A small smile crept out on his face. "I didn't mean any offense. He obviously trusts you. And I can see why."

Olivia frowned. "What do you mean?"

Trent gestured back to the open door, beyond which they could hear Terra's soft sobs. "I've seen grown alpha male wolves quiver under one of Terra's freak out assaults. This one tonight was *epic*, and you completely kept your cool. *And you're human.*" He paused to give her a heart-stopping smile. "If Riverwise ever decides to let you go, please let me know. I could use someone who's got a good head about her on my staff."

She was back to blushing again, not least because Trent seemed to mean every word. And he had no reason to flatter her, none that she could see, anyway. "Staff? What kind of work do you do?"

His smile tempered a little, but he seemed pleased that she was asking. "Software development. But we have a need for all sorts on the payroll. The company's rapidly growing, and I'm always on the hunt for talent. Tell me, Ms. Lilyfield, what kind of work would you *like* to do?"

The coffeepot sputtered next to them. Olivia could hardly believe Trent was trying to recruit her in the middle of this crisis to find his sister, but maybe that was how they did things in the Wilding pack. The least she could do was make distracting small talk until Jaxson had some real news for them.

She just prayed that would be soon.

CHAPTER 9

"So, you and Olivia, huh?" Jace's voice was barely above a whisper.

They were hunched outside a warehouse at the outskirts of Seattle. A little drawn blood and one good bite had convinced the broken-nosed thug to give up the location where the shifters were transported to—the only question was whether Cassie was inside or not. And, if so, how they were going to infiltrate it. They'd left the thug unconscious with his friend so he wouldn't be ratting them out. Right now, they were waiting for Murphy, Taylor, and Rich to scout the perimeter and report back with options.

"Focus, Jace," Jaxson said. "We're on a mission, remember?"

"I'm just saying... I didn't see that coming." Jace moved his weight from one foot to the other, easing his muscles. They were crouched behind the natural shrubbery next to the electrified, razor-wire fence surrounding the warehouse. A single guard inhabited the shack next to the gate, but even taking him down wouldn't necessarily gain them entrance.

"Unless the men can find an alternate entry point, I'm thinking the shack is our best option. But we need the guard alive if we're going to gain a passcode."

"Agreed." Jace stretched his arms, limbering up. "I still think I can clear the fence, though. Or just take it out." His brother had enhanced shifter abilities, beyond what most wolves possessed. But shifting for him was... unpredictable. And potentially very dangerous, for everyone—including Jace himself.

"I don't like that option." Jaxson peered around the back of the bush, but still no sign of his pack. "Plus I didn't bring the appropriate supplies for that."

"Last resort, then," Jace said, dipping his head.

Jaxson nodded. He would take the chance in using Jace's abilities if he had to. None of them wanted Cassie trapped inside that building one second longer than necessary.

Jace leaned over to bump Jaxson's shoulder with his. "So... our new *office assistant* is working out for you, huh?"

"Can we not talk about this right now?" Jaxson growled. He couldn't believe his willpower had failed him so utterly, so soon. His wolf was howling for her, but that was no excuse. It was the *man* in him who couldn't resist her curves. Or her bravery. Or her sweet, sweet mouth. He still hadn't deciphered that electric jolt he got every time he touched her, but after the agony of the date with Morrigan, the breath-of-fresh-air that was Olivia had been way too much temptation for him.

Jace chuckled, low and quiet. "I think we need to talk about the proper use of Riverwise office furniture—"

"Shut up."

"Hey, I have to work there, too." Jace's harassment was clearly just getting started. "But if you've got a taste for humans now, I've got several who—"

Jaxson whipped his hand to his brother's throat. *"Shut. It."*

Jace's eyes were wide with surprise, not fear. "Okay, then," he said in a strained way around Jaxson's hold on his throat. Jaxson released him, but Jace's expression just went straight to *Jaxson has lost his marbles.*

"I guess we'll talk about this later," Jace said carefully.

"Later." Jaxson checked his weapon. *Much later.* All of it would eventually come out. Right now, they really *did* need to focus on getting back this kidnaped shifter girl. The whole thing ran icicles through his heart—this was a change in the game, whatever game had been going on before with the shifter disappearances. And he didn't like it one bit.

Thankfully, an almost-silent scuffle in the dirt behind him signaled the return of his three pack members from surveillance.

"What do you have for me?" Jaxson asked.

Murphy hunched next to him. "Razor-wire all around. Electrification is solid."

"I'd have to go back for the right equipment to take down the fence," Taylor added.

"No time for that," Jaxson said.

There was agreement and frowns all around.

Jaxson sighed. "All right, the guard. Same drill as before. Murphy, we need him conscious."

"You got it, boss." He shifted his claws in and out.

Maybe Jaxson would let Murphy take point in tormenting the passcode out of the guard. Jaxson did what he had to, but he took no pleasure from it. And he'd already had his fill for the night.

"Okay, we'll have to make this fast. Once we take the shack, Taylor works the control system from the inside.

Maybe we can get access that way. Murphy, you go to work on the guard. Jace, Rich, and I will get ready for whatever's going to storm out of the warehouse once we attack. I'm sure they've got—"

The crunch of car tires interrupted him. A beam of headlights swept across the shrubbery in front of them. Everyone dropped to a tighter crouch in their hiding spot, while Jaxson peered through the branches, searching for the source. A white van pulled to a stop at the guard shack.

"White van." Jace's voice was low and tight. That's all they had for a description of the vehicle used to snatch Cassie, but it was enough.

"New plan," Jaxson said to all of them. "Get that goddamned van before it breaches the gate. *Go.*"

The five of them sprung from their hiding spot and raced toward the van and the guard who had just stepped out of his shack. Murphy and Rich shifted mid-sprint, using their wolf forms to run faster and get there first. Their black coats and silent paws meant the guard barely had warning before they descended upon him in a flurry of midnight fur and fangs. Jaxson took the driver's side while Taylor went passenger-side. Jace bee-lined to the back door of the van. The ripping sound of claws going through steel tore through the night just as Jaxson arrived at the driver's still-open window. One solid fist to the face put the driver down. Taylor had him covered with his gun from the passenger side, but there was no need. Jaxson waved him off. Then he pulled open the door and dragged the driver out into the dirt.

A scream from the guard drew Jaxson's attention. Murphy had the man's throat in his jaws, and Rich had clamped down on a leg. The scream must have been from that, but the guard wasn't struggling. He seemed to realize he wasn't dead yet, but Murphy could make him that way if he moved. Jaxson pulled his weapon and pointed it at the guard's head, just in case.

"Jace!" Jaxson called to the back of the van. "What do we have?"

"I've got her!" Jace yelled from inside the van. That was followed by a muffled whimper and Jace's voice dropped to soft and reassuring.

Liquid relief flushed through Jaxson's body. On the heels of that emotion came the need to shoot the driver lying in the dust as well as the prone guard. But he resisted. Dead bodies with his pack's DNA all over them? Not worth the sweet taste of revenge.

A klaxon sound roared through the air, and million-watt spotlights sprung to life outside the warehouse. Black shapes spilled from a side door.

Shit.

"Everyone in the van!" Jaxson shouted.

JAXSON

Bullets pinged the ground, and Taylor went down in the dirt on the passenger side. *Goddammit.* Jaxson climbed into the driver's side and army-crawled across the bench to reach the passenger door. Glass from the windshield shattered as a bullet found a home there. Jaxson flung open the door. Taylor was down but still moving. Jaxson reached down and hauled him up into the cab. A glance up showed the paramilitary guys who had disgorged from the warehouse were held up at the still-closed gate. They couldn't touch it—one was screaming orders for it to open up while the others sent a spray of bullets thunking into the van. Jaxson felt one clip his arm before he managed to duck behind the cover of the dash.

"Jace! Are we clear?" Jaxson shouted over the sound of ripping metal and bullet retorts.

"Clear! Clear! Clear!" Jace yelled, which meant Murphy and Rich must have made it into the back of the van.

Jaxson threw the van in reverse and floored it. He was driving blind, but he had to put distance between the van and the gate before the reinforcements managed to get it open. He mapped the terrain from memory, remembering the slight curve in the dirt road just before it reached the warehouse and how it met up with the paved city road. A hard bounce told him he'd reached the pavement, so he cranked the wheel, which brought the lit-up warehouse into view through the side window.

The gate was just starting to spring open.

Jaxson popped upright in the driver's seat, slammed the brakes, then shoved the van into drive. Another hard turn brought him around facing the right direction to make their escape, peeling rubber but accelerating as fast as the lumbering rental van could manage. It felt like driving through molasses compared to the bullets still biting the ground and pinging the metal of the van, but after ten, long heart-stopping seconds, they reached another turn in the road. He took it as fast as he could without rolling the van.

He knew they were out of line-of-sight when the bullets stopped finding them.

"Fuck," said Taylor, struggling to sit up in the passenger seat.

"You all right?" Jaxson asked. It came out as a gasp—his lungs were struggling for oxygen, just now catching up to the adrenaline pumping through his system with a heart beating twice as fast as normal.

"Yeah." Taylor sounded disappointed. And his voice held very little strain for as much blood as was running down his front. "This was one of my favorite shirts."

Jaxson let out a chuckle. "You're such an ass."

Taylor looked offended. "It was a present from my mom."

JAXSON

Jaxson grinned. "Jace?" he called to the back. "What's our status?"

Silence.

Jaxson's grin fell off his face. Icy hands clenched his heart. "Jace!"

His brother popped his head through the opening in the glass window between the cab and the back of the van. "Keep your pants on. Everything's fine."

Jaxson breathed a sigh of relief and shook his head. "Injuries?"

"Murphy took a bullet. He's complaining like a baby, but it's nothing."

"Could be mortal!" Murphy's voice echoed through the van. "I might be dying here!"

Jaxson gave his brother a quizzical look.

"He's playing it up for Cassie," Jace said with an unimpressed look.

Jaxson rolled his eyes, then asked in a quieter voice, "How is she?"

Jace grinned. "I found her kicking the shit out of her guard when I opened the back."

Jaxson snorted a laugh that almost choked him. "Well, she *is* a Wilding."

Jace gave an appreciative look over his shoulder. "They grow 'em feisty in that pack." Then he swung his gaze back to Jaxson and smirked. "I'm sure her big sister will be *very* appreciative when we get back."

Jaxson didn't answer, just scowled then turned forward to drive the van.

His heart was still racing—the adrenaline mixed with the exhilaration of recovering the girl—but they were far from done with this. Tonight, they'd stopped whoever was hunting shifters from getting *this* little girl, but there was no telling who else was in that damn warehouse. Or what torments they were enduring. And if these bastards were bold enough to grab Cassie off the street, then they had to know the Wildings were shifters. Or at least the branch of the pack with Cassie's family. Which mean Terra, Trent, and Cassie's father were in danger, too. Hopefully, they had realized that already and had gone to Riverwise for safe keeping.

"Get on the phone, Jace," he called back without taking his eyes off the road. "Tell them we're bringing Cassie back to the office. And *not* to go home."

"On it." Jace's voice muffled when he closed the window to the cab, but Jaxson could still make out the pauses and rhythm of his voice. It was no doubt Olivia on the other end, standing by for news that they'd recovered the girl. When he heard Cassie's muffled voice come through from the back of the van, Jaxson grinned. Terra must have shown up at the office, just like he expected. Which meant he'd left Olivia there to deal with that hot mess all on her own.

He owed her. Big time.

And he'd deal with the mess when they got back.

CHAPTER 10

Olivia couldn't believe how relieved she felt when Jaxson walked through the door. Jace came first, along with a mini version of Terra that had to be Cassie. They weren't four steps inside before Terra swept Cassie into a fierce hug. Olivia hung back by the corner to the rest of the office. Trent stayed back too, waiting for Terra to go first.

"Oh, Cassie, Cassie." She kept saying the girl's name over and over while clutching her tighter and tighter. The poor thing probably couldn't breathe at all, but her smile lit up every face in the room. Which included Jaxson striding in behind Jace and Cassie, followed closely by his other three pack members, Murphy, Rich, and Taylor.

They were all bloody as hell.

Olivia's mouth dropped open. She had taken the call from Jace, and he had told her they were all right… *but they weren't.* Jaxson's shirt was a torn, bloody mess, and Taylor looked like he'd lost more blood than he owned. Yet they were all striding into the room, laughing and grinning, like everything was fine with the world.

"Tell me they're really okay," Olivia whispered to Trent. He already knew she was a novice with this shifter stuff.

His brilliant smile for the reunion quirked a little to the side. "They're shifters, Olivia. They're fine." Then he stepped forward to embrace his kid sister because Terra had finally let loose her epic hug.

Olivia searched for Jaxson's face, just to see for herself he wasn't as bad off as his shirt portrayed. She found his brilliant blue eyes locked on her from across the room. He beamed a smile for her that made her shoulders relax. Just as he took a step in her direction, Terra popped up between them, cutting off their line of sight. Then she threw her arms around Jaxson, catching him off guard, judging by the startled look on his face.

Olivia's heart sank… but *of course* Terra would want to thank him personally. A set of smirks flitted around the room. Olivia's face grew hot, but she couldn't take her eyes off the pair of them. Jaxson patted Terra's back and whispered something to her while she clung to him, jabbering away with something meant for only Jaxson to hear.

Then Terra pulled back and *kissed him.*

It was no small kiss either—this was a full-body embrace, tongue-to-tongue, Terra's hands clutching Jaxson's head and pulling his mouth to hers with what looked like all her shifter strength.

Olivia dropped her gaze to the carpet by her feet. Her face was on fire with embarrassment. She should leave. *Immediately.* That much was clear.

Jace was suddenly at her side. "Okay, then. Time for us to go." He threw an arm around her shoulders and steered her away from the front entryway, around the corner to the main part of the office. Olivia let him, simply because she was numb and couldn't think of anything to say or do differently.

Once they were around the corner, she pulled out of his hold. "I… um… I should get my things."

"Olivia," Jace said, voice laden with apology. "You have to understand, they're supposed to be mates. It's nothing…" He stopped, looking stricken.

It's nothing personal. That's what he meant to say before he stopped himself. Olivia was sure of it. Her heart was banging itself into pieces inside her chest. It physically *hurt*. She pressed a hand over her heart, sure that something was actually happening inside there. Like she was having a legit heart attack over this. Over a gorgeous man who kissed her twice but never belonged to her.

She fought back the tears and slowly looked up from the floor.

Jace's grimace turned even more pained at her expression.

"It's all right," she said, as much to herself as to him. "I'll be fine. I just need to… get a few of my things."

"Olivia—" Jace tried to stop her, but she evaded his arms and stumbled toward her office.

Out of the corner of her eye, she saw Jaxson striding in from the entryway, but she just ducked her head and kept going. The only way she could make it through this was to get to her office, pull herself together, gather up her things, and *get out*. She could break down, have a good, long heart-breaking sob-fest over ice cream in her apartment, where no one would see.

But not until then.

The tears receded as she reached her office door and strode inside. She swung the door shut behind her and kept walking, but then she stopped short when it didn't bang closed. She turned to check, but Jaxson was already there, catching it before it could slam shut.

"Olivia—" He had a horrified look on his face.

She put up a hand to stop him. "It's all right. Really." She dropped her gaze to her desk drawer so she could fish out her wallet, keys, and phone. There was nothing else she needed to take with her, and she certainly wasn't coming back.

"It's not all right—"

"No, you're right," she cut him off again. She could feel the anger rising, but she fought it back down just as she scooped her things out of the drawer and straightened up to face him.

He had closed the door behind him, but the stricken look was still on his face.

"You completely went off plan," she said, mock-chastising him with a shake of her finger. "Dating Terra wasn't supposed to happen until *next* week." She had to look away because the pained look on his face was too much for her. She stared at the images of the three shifter women still open on her computer instead. "Anyway, brilliant work. You didn't need me after all. Not when you could be a hero and save Terra's little sister. I mean, who could resist that—"

His hand was on her elbow. "Olivia." His voice was soft and close.

She couldn't do this much longer. She set her things on the desk, turned to him, and stared up into his

JAXSON

gorgeous blue eyes with as much fortitude as she could muster. "It's all right. I won't embarrass you." She was proud that her voice wasn't trembling as much as she was afraid it might, especially with him so close. "It's obviously time for me to leave, but I'll be okay. Trent's offered me a job, so you don't have to worry about that."

"Oh, did he now?" Jaxson hadn't backed off an inch. In fact, he was edging even closer, gazing down into her eyes with a soft expression that was stabbing her in the chest again. "Well, Trent is a slimy womanizing beta that I wouldn't allow near *any* female. No way am I letting him steal you away."

Her mouth fell open. "Well, I have to work *somewhere*. Some of us don't have successful businesses rolling in celebrity money, you know!"

"You're working *here*. For *me*." He was so close now, he was practically, but not quite, touching her in three different places: his hands lingering near her balled up fists; his breath mingling with hers; and his broad, muscular body nearly making contact with her chest, which was heaving with the emotion ripping through it.

"Jaxson," she said, her voice pained. "I know our kiss didn't mean anything to you, but I can't—"

He cut her off with his lips crashing down on her. It was fast and hungry and stole her breath... but it was over in an instant. His hands locked on her wrists and pulled her body against his. His lips weren't touching hers any longer, but he was close enough to exchange heated breaths. Her heart hammered her chest, soaring with something like hope, but still horribly uncertain. Afraid to believe it was real.

"Terra means nothing to me," he whispered. "Terra. Thea. Morrigan. None of them will *ever* mean anything to me. *You*, on the other hand... how about I show you just how much I want you to stay?" He cupped her cheeks in his large, strong hands and gently kissed her lips, once, twice, a half dozen times. But what he was really doing was turning her around so her bottom was pressed against the hard edge of the desk.

"I think this is about where we left off," he whispered. Then he skimmed his hands down her body, touching her and lighting her on fire as he went, until he reached her hips—which he hoisted up on the desk, forcing her legs apart with his body. "And this is where I planned to go next."

"Jaxson," she protested, but her body was responding to him already. Growing hot and wet, begging for his touch. "Everyone's just outside."

"I told Jace to take them to the safehouse." He kissed her quickly and leaned back to pull off his bloody and ruined shirt.

She couldn't help sucking in a breath. The full expanse

of his muscled chest was on display for her, begging her to touch him. She slid her fingertips along the words tattooed across his chest—*omni tempore*—but she had no idea what they meant. Something about time? And he had another tattoo, a wolf on his shoulder. But her attention was quickly drawn to the blood-smeared part of his arm.

She gently touched the ridge of pinkish skin, a fresh scar, then looked into his eyes. "Please tell me you've magically healed from whatever this was."

"I've magically healed from the bullet wound." He pressed her hand flat against his shoulder, on top of the scar, then dragged her hand across his chest, holding her fingers flat against his skin. She could feel him rumbling pleasure at her touch deep inside his chest. Then he drew her hand down. Her eyes went wide as he pressed her palm against his rock-hard erection. "But I'm going to need your help with this."

Breath escaped her. She moved her hand against his cock. It strained against the fabric of his dress pants.

He groaned and snatched her hand away. "On second thought, that will have to wait." He slid her further onto the desk, hiking up her skirt and spreading her legs wide. Then he ran a hand up her body to her hair, pulling it gently to tip her head back and expose her neck. He nipped kisses from her collarbone to her jaw, causing heat to gush between her legs. Then he devoured her lips with his kiss, plunging into her mouth and making demands of it.

She was open to him, completely, wholly. She wanted nothing more than for him to take her *right now,* but he was slowly, luxuriously plundering her mouth with his tongue while his hands skimmed her breasts, teasing and squeezing by turns. It was getting hard to breathe.

Were they doing this? Were they *really* doing this? She didn't know if it made any sense, or if Jaxson meant what he said—that he would never want the women he should be taking for a mate—but he hadn't lied to her yet. And even if this moment was all they would ever have, she wasn't going to say no. Not when this could be part of her life—*he* could be part of her life—even for a short time before it all came crashing down in heartbreak.

He finally pulled free of the long, breathless exploration of her mouth. His eyes were blazing blue fire, and his hands were on her hips, pulling her closer to the edge of the desk. His raging hard-on pressed against her inner thigh. So close… and yet not close enough. Not for what she really wanted.

"Olivia." He was panting as hard as she was. "I'm dying to taste you."

"I think you just did," she said with a ghost of a smile.

A quick smirk flashed across his face, but it was

replaced just as fast by a hungry look so intense, it made fresh heat flush between her legs.

"That's not what I meant." His hands slid down her thighs and slipped under her hiked-up skirt. He shoved it up farther, and his large hands sought out the fabric of her underwear. She startled as he literally *ripped* her underwear in half. Then he dropped to one knee and pulled her leg over his shoulder.

Oh, God, was he…

"I want to *taste* you." He licked his lips and dove between her legs.

She gasped as his tongue flicked across her tender flesh… tasting… testing… *Oh God, he was going down on her.* She pulsed with need for him, and he responded by pulling her tighter to his lips, using every tool at his disposal—lips, teeth, and tongue, oh God that glorious tongue—to flush waves of pleasure through her. Every touch jolted with electric pleasure. She grasped the back of his head, urging him deeper. He plunged his tongue inside her, making her whimper. Her other hand braced against the desk as her head tipped back, and small moans worked out of her throat. She was breathing so hard, she was becoming light-headed, but he kept working her body, flicking shocks across her tight nub. Tension coiled low in her belly, and she could feel it coming—an orgasm like none she'd ever felt.

"Oh, God, Jaxson," she moaned. *"Please."*

He didn't answer, just hummed his pleasure against her most sensitive parts, making her shriek a little with the intensity. Then he moved slightly upward, and she had the crazy thought that he might leave her hanging there, right on the precipice, tormented… but then he thrust two fingers inside her.

She gasped at the suddenness of it, and the pleasure. He kept his tongue flicking her nub, but then he started pumping his fingers, faster and faster, building the pleasure so tight and hard, she couldn't keep it inside. She bucked against him and came on his hand, moaning and shrieking the entire time. She rode and rode his fingers, wrenching every bit of pleasure from them. When her body finally slowed its convulsive waves, the orgasm passing like a quieting storm, Jaxson pulled back and pulled out, taking his red-hot tongue and fingers with him.

He stood and locked gazes with her. "You are so goddamn hot, Olivia." He practically tore off his belt, then shoved his pants and underwear down, springing his cock free. It was so large, so perfectly thick and long, Olivia couldn't do anything but stare. She was breathing too hard to say anything coherent.

He stroked himself once, then twice. "Take a good long look. Because you won't see this again for a while—

JAXSON

I plan on burying it inside you for a good, long time."

An embarrassing whimper escaped her, but *Oh my God*. What did he expect, saying things like that? Then he moved fast, grabbing her ankles and hoisting them up to his shoulders so that she was forced to lie back on the table. He bent over her, his enormous cock teasing her entrance but not burying inside her, like he promised. Instead, he took his time unbuttoning her blouse. To her amazement, a claw slowly grew from one of his fingers and neatly sliced through her bra, liberating her breasts from their restraints. They bobbed on her chest, and he groaned, holding them with both hands. His eyes were half-lidded with lust.

"You're everything I want, Olivia," he breathed as he worked the globes of her breasts. "Everything I need." He trailed his fingers down her body, hooking them under the waist of her skirt and leaning back to pull it free. She was nearly naked now, as was he. He slid his cock tantalizingly along the hyper-sensitive flesh of between her legs, but still refused to enter and take her the way she wanted.

"What I can't figure out," he said, breath short. "Is what I can do for you."

"I can think of one thing," she panted and gave him a wide-eyed *why are you waiting?* look.

He smirked, and then his expression went hungry, a

look that sent shivers racing through her. He pressed the head of his cock against her entrance while leaning over her to bore that look of desire straight into her eyes.

"Is this what you want?" he asked, still teasing her.

"God, Jaxson, *please.*" She grasped at his hands, which were holding her hips motionless so she couldn't buck against him.

He sighed his pleasure. "I just wanted to hear you beg, sweet Olivia."

Then he eased his cock into her, slowly and teasingly but *oh freaking God* he was so big. He stretched and filled her like no man had before. Her back arched, and she moaned uncontrollably. Then he slid almost completely out and thrust back in *fast*. She gasped, but it was nothing like the moans of pleasure rumbling in his chest. After a few rapid, hard thrusts—and she gloried in all their power—he slipped into a rhythm that was just right. The pressure was building fast inside her, and before she could catch her breath, she was rocketing toward another orgasm.

"Jaxson," she panted. "Oh, God, Jaxson, I'm going to..."

"Come for me, baby," he said, voice tight. "I want to feel you come undone around me."

His words pushed her over the edge, and her body convulsed, waves of pleasure so extreme washing through her that she was certain she'd passed out and traveled into some other realm filled with nothing but body-wracking pleasure, electric touches, and love.

Love.

Even as her body was completely owned by the pleasure he was thrusting inside her, Olivia's heart soared, connecting with him, belonging to him. In a moment of ecstasy-fueled delirium, she could see that first touch, that first time his lips touched her skin and the electric feel of them… that was the moment when she truly became his. All the rest was just discovering that truth. And now, at the height of her pleasure, she was fully and completely aware of that fact.

Jaxson River was the only man who would ever be *this* to her.

When she started to come down, and awareness of the world faded back, she realized Jaxson was still slowly moving in and out of her. Still rock-hard. She opened her eyes and scanned his face.

It was lit with joy. "Dammit woman, you are so beautiful." He slid out of her, and she immediately missed the fullness. And the sense of connection. He gathered her hands in his and pulled her up to sitting. "Come with me," he said, and she nodded.

She would go anywhere with this man.

Chapter 11

Watching Olivia come as Jaxson pounded his cock into her was practically a religious experience. Her gorgeous curves, the look on her face, the extreme pleasure of her pulsing around him—it was all so intense, he could barely keep from coming himself. And the electric feel of every part of her, every time he touched her, no matter where, no matter how... it was like the universe was connecting through them, binding them together.

He wanted to draw all of this out as long as possible.

Jaxson eased her off the desk. She blinked—a lot—

and he couldn't contain his smile at pleasuring her so thoroughly that it left her obviously light-headed. And he wanted to do *so much more.*

"Come sit in the chair with me," he said with a grin. He reached back to pull the wide leather chair underneath him. Then he guided her toward him, drawing her knees up, one at a time until she was straddling him on the chair. He edged forward, positioning his cock right at her entrance, then slowly eased her down on him, burying himself inside her once again.

He groaned. *This.* This was where he wanted to be. *Always.*

Her eyes were wide, but she quickly got the idea. She grasped the back of the chair, angled him deeper, and rode him like a champion—slowly at first, then edging faster, bit by bit.

Holy fuck. He wanted to watch her sweet body swallow him whole, but that was going to push him over the edge even faster. He closed his eyes, leaned his head back, and groaned through the pleasure.

"Are you okay?" She was breathless and concerned, her fingertips gently touching his face. He opened his eyes. Her flushed-pink, puckered-nipple body was riding him like the rise and fall of a decadent merry-go-round— only he got to be a very lucky horse.

"Am I okay?" He gasped in between the words. "A goddess is riding me... so no, I think I might actually die in this moment. Die a very happy man."

She smiled, and it made her even more beautiful. Then, in the middle of driving him insane, she trailed her fingers across his chest, and asked, "What does it mean?"

She meant his tat—*omni tempore*. "It's from the SEALs. *All in, all the time.*" He smirked and thrust up to meet her on the downward stroke, driving his cock even deeper inside her... which just made him suck in a breath as it forced a gasp from her. "Not quite what my CO meant at the time."

Her smile grew even wider. He wanted to stay *all in, all the time* with her—wanted to give her everything he had to give—but that grin of hers was too much. He needed to touch her, pound into her, and banish that smile with more screams of pleasure. He lifted the heavy globe of her silken breast with one hand, and pressed the other to her sex, slick between them. Every touch sparked with that special something that he'd only ever experienced with *her*. He worked that for everything it was worth, giving her as much as he was getting. She started to pump faster, but *oh God*... that would make him come, and he couldn't have that. Not yet. This was too much perfection, too much of everything he'd ever wanted—all the connection he never thought he would have outside a true mating—and he wanted to stretch it out as long as it could possibly go.

He flicked his thumb faster over her nub. She gasped and bucked against him, her delicate fingers digging into his shoulders. She shuddered, perking her nipple in his hand… and then she came undone around him, squeezing his cock with her orgasm in a way that nearly drove him to the edge. Before she was even finished, he had to lift her off, or that would end it right there.

He gently placed her on her feet and held her up because she didn't quite have her legs yet. His voice was hoarse with need for her. He whispered into her hair, "I want to bend you over my desk and take you from behind. Please, God, say yes."

She didn't answer, just twisted out of his arms and prostrated herself on his desk, sending her phone and keys crashing to the floor. She was offering her gorgeous body to him, exposed and waiting, looking over her shoulder with a half-lidded look of pure desire.

He grabbed her hips and slammed into her, just as he'd dreamed of doing since he first laid eyes on her. Her muffled cry sent even more satisfaction coursing through him, and he kept thrusting, slamming harder, losing his mind in this moment. His mouth watered, and his fangs came out. His wolf howled in triumph and growled in his need to claim her. He wanted to make her his forever.

This was how it should be—her giving herself over to him so freely, him taking her higher than she'd ever gone, him claiming her with his bite and his love.

His love.

Goddammit. He was so in love with this woman. Not being able to claim her—never being able to have her, not like that, not bound magically—hurt like nothing he'd ever known. He pushed that aside and picked up his pace, finally allowing himself to rush toward that climax he prayed wouldn't be the end—the end of this hasty tryst; the end of her giving herself wholly and freely to him. He prayed when he told her the truth, that he could still keep her, even if she wasn't the mate his wolf dreamed of and howled for.

Olivia screamed his name as she came, and that tripped him over the edge with her. Pleasure coursed through him and chased away the worry, just for a single, glorious moment that stretched and stretched. He kept rocking into her until the last waves of her orgasm had subsided. Then he drew her up into his arms and folded her into his lap on the chair again. He kissed all over her beautiful face.

"Olivia, Olivia." He said her name over and over, hoping that would press upon her the depth of his feelings. Such a short time since she had come into his life, and already she had completely upended it. Laid bare how empty it was. How much he had let the curse ruin living for him.

The curse.

It was time to tell her the truth.

Her breathing was still ragged, as was his, but he didn't want to wait any longer.

"Olivia." He stroked her cheek and lifted her chin so she would look up at him and not just snuggle into his chest. Although that feeling of *completeness*—of connection—was exactly what he hoped they would continue to have. *Forever.* If she would let him.

"Yes?" She peered up into his eyes, a smile glowing on her face, and he couldn't resist kissing her once more, just lightly.

"I need to tell you something."

Her eyes went slightly wide, then she dropped her gaze to his chest again. "Okay," she said, but there was a new tremor in her voice that he didn't care for *at all*.

He frowned and adjusted her in his lap so he could see her face. "I have a secret I've been keeping from you."

This made her face draw down, like she was afraid to hear it. That stabbed into him, but she didn't say anything more.

He stroked her cheek again. "Don't take it personally. I've been keeping this secret from everyone for a long time." He couldn't help a sardonic smile at how true that was.

That seemed to banish some of the fear in her eyes. "Then why are you telling it to *me?*"

His smile grew. "Because it affects you. Because you're part of it? Because there's something about you that made me realize that keeping this secret even one more day was stopping me from actually living my life."

That perked her interest considerably. She looked at him with something like wonder and gently touched her beautiful fingers to his face. "Whatever your secrets are, Jaxson River, I promise to keep them."

"That's just it." His smile dimmed a little. "I don't want to keep it anymore." He drew in a deep breath and let the words just tumble out. "I've been cursed, Olivia. A long time ago, when I was barely old enough to drive, a witch laid a curse on me that would forever change my life."

She drew back, horror on her face. "A witch?"

"I told you they sometimes went after female shifters, right?"

Olivia nodded, but the horror-stricken look on her face just grew.

"Well, this one wanted my heart as well—or at least my body, as a slave to hers. I found out later that it's much more common than I knew."

JAXSON

"I don't understand," Olivia said, but her face had lost color, and her body was tensed up into a tight ball. "She wanted you for a slave?"

Jaxson hated seeing the tension rivet her body, so he rushed through the rest of the explanation. "She wanted me for *sex*. It's a thing with some female witches, I don't know why, but they're attracted to male shifters and want to turn them into sexual slaves. The witch's magic is powerful enough to make it possible. Typically, the wolf doesn't survive. She uses him for sex until she's bored, then she bleeds him of his magic-filled blood. It's a degrading and horrible way to die." He took a breath, but pressed on. The look on Olivia's face was becoming more horrified by the moment. "Anyway, I was young and stupid, and I didn't know I was playing with fire. I slept with her a few times because… I couldn't help myself. I was a horny young wolf and witches are preternaturally hot—their beauty spells are unbelievable. Anyway, when she said she wanted to keep me—as in *keep me for a sex toy*—I finally wised up and told her no. Only, by that point, I think she was in love with me. Or something. Maybe she just really didn't like her pet talking back." He paused. "She said I was too pretty to kill, so she cursed me instead. The spell poisoned the magic in my blood. If I ever take a mate, if I ever complete the mating ritual with a bite that transfers my magic to the woman I love… she'll die."

He had hoped the horror would fade once Olivia realized what that meant—that he could never have a mate and that all of this search for a shifter female was just a ruse—but the look of revulsion just solidified into a deep sadness.

"That's horrible," she said quietly, staring at his chest. "How could someone do that to a another person?"

"I told you before: witches aren't normal people. They're basically evil walking around on sexy-hot legs."

Olivia looked up at that, but her lips were trembling. "Are they all that way?"

He frowned. "All the ones I've met. Or heard of." It was an odd question, though—and not the one he expected. "But don't you see? This means I *can't* have a mate. I'm never going to be with another shifter, no matter how much my inner wolf wants that to happen."

"Jaxson, I'm… I'm sorry." Her voice was so laden with heartbreak, he could hardly stand it.

He pulled her closer into his arms. "It not your fault, sweet, sweet Olivia," he whispered into her hair. Then he pulled back and smiled, trying to lift her out of this despair she seemed to have fallen into. "And I'm finally realizing that, even if I can't have a mate, maybe I can still have something just as precious."

His smile wasn't having any effect on her.

JAXSON

"Why haven't you told anyone about this?" she asked. "I mean, it's not your fault you can't have a mate. People should understand."

His smile faded. "Sure. They'll understand. They'll see immediately that I'm an alpha who can never take a mate. And an alpha without a mate is one who can't have pups. Can't carry on the line of the pack. And that's an alpha who *can't lead.*"

"Can't lead?" Olivia scrunched up her nose. "Why? You're this amazing, brave, selfless man. Why would they care if you have a mate or not?"

The tension in Jaxson's shoulders released. *Damn,* he loved this woman. She saw straight to the heart of things and wasn't afraid to speak it.

"I know," he said softly. "But it's how the pack operates. The mating ritual isn't just taking a wife—it's a magical bond that literally makes the alpha stronger. And the pack is stronger for it, too. If I can't fulfill that role, I *should* step aside and let someone else do it. The only problem has been…"

Her eyes widened with understanding. "Jared. He can't take a mate either."

"Right." Jaxson shrugged. "He has a good reason, but the fact remains just the same."

"What about Jace?" Her eyes were alive with hope now.

Jaxson sucked in a breath. "Jace has his own issue. One that... well, let's just say it would be extremely difficult for him to take a mate. And Jace would never risk it. *Never.* And I can't blame him there." He shrugged. "Three brothers, and not one of us able to deliver the goods."

Olivia's frown was back, and her gaze dropped to her hands, which were wringing each other. "This is why everyone wants you to take a mate." She looked up at him. "Because they don't know about the curse. And you're the only brother who can."

"Right." He gave her a soft smile. "And as soon as they know, the Riverwise pack is going to fall apart. I might be able to hold them together for a little while, but it will be a terrible blow. And with the disappearances happening, we can't afford that. Plus we need to keep our alliances with the other packs strong so we can stop whoever is taking the shifters. Especially now that they're targeting our packs directly."

She nodded. "You need to keep this under wraps. Until that can be handled, at least."

His smile brightened. "Exactly." He ran a finger along her lips. "And once that's settled, once we've figured out who's threatening us and dispensed with them, then the danger will be past. And I'll be free to tell the truth." He paused, then took the leap. "I'll be free to be with you."

Her eyes went wide. "But I'm human."

He moved his finger to tracing a line along her cheek, up to tuck a stray piece of hair, set loose by their lovemaking, behind her ear. "That doesn't matter to me. I want to be with *you*, Olivia."

But instead of embracing him or at least smiling, her frown came back, and she scrambled out of his lap. "You're an amazing, wonderful man, Jaxson," she said, trembling as she stood before him, naked and standing tall. "But I can't be with you. Not like that."

He frowned and a stabbing pain ran through his chest. He quickly rose up from the chair to stand with her. "I don't understand. I thought…" He glanced at the desk. Hadn't they just made love? Was he imagining the beautiful connection between them with every touch? "I thought you *wanted* this."

Her face scrunched up and tears glassed her eyes. "I… I…" She was grasping for words, and he couldn't help—he was completely confused.

He took her trembling shoulders in his hands. "What is it? What's wrong?" He searched her face, but all he saw was fear and pain and… grief. He didn't understand it at all.

She sucked in a deep breath and pulled out of his grasp. She was still trembling. "This was… having sex with you was… very nice. But I can't be with you, Jaxson.

I'm in love with someone else."

"What?" His mouth hung open.

She just ducked her head and scrambled to gather up her clothes. Some of them were in tatters, but she managed to shove on her skirt and pull her blouse closed with a button or two.

He gaped at her. This was all unraveling, and he didn't understand any of it. *"Who* are you in love with?" he managed to get out. He was still standing naked in the middle of her office and watching her hurry around to pick up her things.

"It's no one you know." Then she looked like she was going to run straight out the door.

He rushed over to beat her to it, holding it closed. *"Olivia...* what are you talking about? I thought... I didn't think there was anyone else in your life."

Tears were running down her face, but her face twisted in anger. Anger that she threw at *him.* "There's *not.* Not really. And there never will be for me, just like with you. Only my problem isn't magical at all, just stupid, stupid human love. I fell for a man who can never be mine."

"I don't understand." Truer words had never been spoken. Jaxson's entire body deflated with the misery of this.

"He's *married,* okay?" she shouted. "He's a millionaire

with the perfect life and a wife he'll never give up for me. I'll never be more than an occasional fling for him, but I can't help loving him anyway. *There!* Are you happy? You know my secret. Now let me go!" She gestured angrily at the door, tears gushing down her cheeks as she demanded that he let her run away half-dressed and bawling.

He stepped aside, mouth still hanging open.

She tore open the door and fled the office.

He just stood and watched her go.

Her bare feet pounded the carpet as she ran... and his heart shattered more with each step.

CHAPTER 12

Lies. All of it complete lies.

Olivia had no idea where she conjured this whopper about being in love with a married man—it just spilled from her mouth as her mind was spinning with all the truths Jaxson was telling her. He was *cursed*. By a *witch*. Some vile vixen wanted his body and cursed his heart when she couldn't have it.

If Jaxson discovered Olivia was part witch, he wouldn't simply gape at her, bewildered, like when she left him in her office less than a minute ago. *He would hate her.* And rightly so... because her kind had ruined his life.

And the curse of one witch might take down all of Riverwise, too. Not to mention endanger all the shifters who were being kidnapped. Who would rescue them, if Jaxson's pack was crippled? They needed a leader they could believe in, not one who was weakened by the fact that he couldn't take a mate.

Or that he'd had sex with a witch on the office furniture.

She balled up her fist and pounded it against the wall of the elevator, again and again. It wasn't fair. Not to Jaxson, and not even fair to her. She knew she could never get close to someone, not the way Jaxson wanted, but she'd never had anyone come into her life and make her want that *so badly*.

She stomped her way across the ground floor. It was dark outside. The drama of the rescue had carried into the night, and then her heart-stopping love-making with Jaxson kept them even later. It had to be past midnight. Her body still thrummed with the pleasure he'd given her, but her face was a sopping mess of tears over having to leave him. But she *had* to… it was better to walk away now before it got any worse. Any more heart-breaking.

She managed to hail a cab even though she could barely see through the tears.

When she got home, she tore off her clothes—they reminded her too much of Jaxson—and crawled into an oversized sweatshirt. Then she curled up in a ball in her bedroom and sobbed until her head ached more than the broken-hearted pain in her chest.

She didn't remember falling asleep.

The next morning flooded her room with light. Every muscle ached, so she dragged herself to the shower and tried to wash away all the salty tears and lovemaking that still clung to her. All traces of Jaxson swirled down the drain.

Her phone buzzed all morning, which she spent eating ice cream and watching whatever was on the free TV channels. And trying to not think about Jaxson and everything she would never have with him. When she finally checked her phone midday, there were a dozen messages from him. She deleted them unread and turned off her phone.

She'd told him she was in love with a man she could never have... and that was true. Only the man was Jaxson. She could never be his mate, and Jaxson *deserved* to have a mate—someone to share that magical bond with and lead his pack with and raise pups with. *Shifter pups.* She couldn't give him that either. Only some kind of half-breed, like she was.

She didn't know how that worked for shifters, but it was dangerous enough with witches. She couldn't even imagine what crossing a half-witch with a full-blooded-shifter would produce. Something unstable for sure. Her half-witch powers certainly were. Unstable. Uncontrollable. Better left stuffed away and unused.

Her mother was a witch; her father was a human; now they were both dead because of her. She couldn't think of any better reason not to mess with the laws of nature than that.

Maybe she should quit Riverwise.

The idea churned her stomach even harder, so she pushed it away.

This was why she never got close to anyone—never *allowed* herself to get too close. She hated to admit it, but she had picked all those loser guys *intentionally*. They were the kind who would cheat on her eventually and give her an easy out. A reason to leave. A reason never to get serious. Because she couldn't afford to love anyone.

Then Jaxson dropped into her life, as unexpected as a thunderstorm on a sunny day. Only she had a dangerous power deep inside her, like a lightning bolt waiting to strike. It had already struck her parents out of the blue, for no reason at all.

Except even that wasn't true.

She had been *angry* with them. She couldn't remember what she had been upset about, but her twelve-year-old self had been really, really *pissed* over something that was probably nothing.

Her mother made no secret about being a witch, and Olivia had tried to please her by learning to conjure spells. She could do the simple things—glamours and spells that curdled milk or rattled cabinets. But anything real—anything powerful—and Olivia had been one big disappointment after another.

Until one day when something... *switched on.*

It was like a lifetime of static buildup discharging all at once. She had turned her parents to ash. Both of them, gone in an instant.

Olivia had huddled over the tiny pile of gray dust that, a moment before, had been the two people she loved most in the world. Aghast. Horrified. Unbelieving that she had done this horrible, terrible thing. If the spell she had unleashed hadn't caught their apartment on fire, Olivia probably would have stayed there, frozen, until she died of hunger or thirst. Or a broken heart. But the fire department came, and the firefighters pulled her from the building.

She didn't remember that part, but people told her about it later. She just woke up in the ambulance, sucking in oxygen through a mask and remembering... remembering that she had killed her parents.

With a power she didn't understand and couldn't control.

So she'd locked it away.

JAXSON

And away it had stayed. Successfully. But there was no way she could afford to get close to someone like that again. And *no way in hell* she was risking the life of someone as brave and good and decent as Jaxson River. She had spent her entire life trying to keep people like him from orbiting into her life… and trying to find a way to make her life count for something. To make up for the past by doing something good with the future.

She thought Riverwise was a place she could do that, but now…

Now she was certain she would have to leave. The sooner the better. Staying would only hurt Jaxson. The sooner she was gone, the sooner he could go back to holding things together and taking care of people and rescuing shifters.

The only problem was that leaving felt like ripping out her heart and stomping on it.

Olivia flicked off the TV and curled tighter on the couch. She let her head fall against the edge of the sofa and closed her eyes. A torrent of emotions swam behind her eyelids. She would need all her resolve to march into Riverwise and quit.

Today was Saturday.

It could wait until Monday.

By then, she would have cried out all her tears.

Chapter 13

Jaxson searched yet another restricted access-only database but still came up empty.

Olivia's digital footprint was incredibly light.

He'd wandered home in a daze after she stormed out of the office, crying and claiming to love another man. His wolf howled at that, jealous and heartbroken, but Jaxson couldn't believe it. He knew she had been hiding something, some dark well of sadness that would bubble up at the strangest of times, but he never figured her for the kind of woman willing to be just something on the side. A fling for some asshole who just wanted her for the hot sex.

His wolf's howl turned to a growl that wanted to tear something limb from limb.

Preferably the asshole.

Jaxson shook his head and focused. He'd only gotten a few hours of sleep, tossing and turning, before he was back in the office, using Riverwise's considerable investigative resources to figure out who the hell Olivia was seeing. He wasn't going to storm up to the guy's house and take him out… probably… but he definitely needed to know what the competition looked like.

And why Olivia was drawn to him.

He'd spent half the morning searching everything he could find on her, but her story just wasn't holding up. Either she was lying or the asshole had supernatural security protocols in place such that he never left a fingerprint on her life. Possible, but everyone slipped up.

And assholes weren't usually that careful.

Jaxson pushed away from his desk where he'd been hunched for an hour. He ran two hands through his hair, took a deep breath, and stretched the aches from his back. It was past noon, and Olivia still wasn't returning his calls. Which meant she was *definitely* ignoring him. He considered a stale sandwich from the vending machines downstairs, but opted to just slam back the half cup of cold coffee he had at the desk. He'd tracked down every facet of Olivia's life that could be gleaned from the public, and less public, databases, and he still had only the barest sketch of her days on the planet.

Foster care. Odd jobs. Tax forms filed, but income too low to pay much in the way of taxes. In fact, he was amazed at how little she got by on. No wonder she was so concerned about the rent. He logged on to Riverwise's account and authorized an advance on her next three paychecks to be direct deposited to her bank today. No matter what happened between them, he wanted to make sure she had some cushion going forward.

The idea that some asshole was bedding her but leaving her vulnerable to being kicked out of her apartment... Jaxson had to shove away from the computer again and pace his office a while to get his rage under control. How could anyone spend more than two minutes with Olivia and not understand how special she was? He would give anything to have the chance to take care of her, and this guy was just...

He stopped his pacing, closed his eyes, and rubbed his temples. *Focus, Jaxson.*

He stalked back to the computer and dove into his research again.

Maybe he didn't go back far enough. Maybe there was some connection in her childhood, before foster care, to this creep. Jaxson had access to even the most confidential files, but it only took a simple search of the newspapers around the time of her placement in foster care to pull up what happened to her parents.

She had told him they were dead. He didn't know they had died in an apartment fire that almost took Olivia's life as well. The official report said the cause of the fire was unknown, but maybe there was something there... some connection that the asshole was holding over her... Jaxson searched the gossip rags and underground newspapers and e-zines. He focused on her parents. Sometimes the most tenuous connections would be whispered in the digital shadows...

Olivia's mother was a witch.

Jaxson's hand froze on the mouse. He'd stumbled into a darknet forum thread titled, *Hunters, Witches, and Other Black Arts*. His search had pinged Rowan Lilyfield in that thread, and it was clear that someone thought Olivia's mother was a witch. There was a whole thread on her: suspected dark art spells performed, a description that matched the other online images he had found of her, and most telling of all... she was raised in a well-known coven on the south side of Seattle. She was a full-blooded witch, although apparently she had married a research professor of some kind rather than taking a male witch for a husband. Then again, male witches were almost as rare as female shifters.

Jaxson slowly lifted his hand from the mouse and leaned back. If Olivia's mother was a witch, then Olivia was at least half witch. But her mother died when Olivia was only twelve… maybe she was never introduced to the dark arts. Either way, the agitation made him rise up from his chair and pace the room.

Did she know? Was she one of them? His mind was a hurricane of confusion and torment. He couldn't square the Olivia he knew—smart and kind, gentle with nervous job applicants, steady head in a crisis—with what he knew to be true about witches. They toyed with shifters like cats with mice. If one of them had gotten inside Riverwise… Olivia now knew all the members of his pack. Could identify them in public. *And* he'd given her detailed information about three *other* packs as well. If she was infiltrating them, secretly working for her mother's coven…

Jaxson stopped dead in his frenetic pacing. An icy dread trickled into his stomach.

What if he was all wrong about Olivia from the start?

He stared out his window at the Seattle skyline and just shook his head slowly. Olivia as an undercover witch invading his pack? That just didn't fit with the tremulous girl he'd made love to last night. Witches were nothing if not sexually experienced—and that's not something a person can easily hide. Either Olivia was an academy

JAXSON

award-winning actress or last night was the first time someone had properly made love to her. Besides, witches used the dark arts to gain advantages in *all* spheres of their lives, including the marketplace. *None* of them worried about the rent.

Jaxson's shoulders relaxed.

The most likely explanation was the simplest. Olivia was exactly what her digital life portrayed—an orphan who scrabbled her way out of foster care and through a series of deadbeat jobs, looking for some kind of meaning in her life. What had she said, that first time, in the library? *My work is important to me.* At the time, he didn't really understand, given she'd just left her job at the paper. But now he could see it—she'd been trying to make something of herself, doing something that *mattered*. That's why she tried to rescue him in the alleyway. And how he'd enticed her to Riverwise in the first place—another chance to help him out of a sticky situation. She'd leapt into that with both feet and stolen his heart in the process.

That was the person Jaxson knew. And loved.

Whatever Olivia's parents had been, they were long dead. She had been surviving on her own ever since, and she deserved better than this mysterious asshole boyfriend who obviously didn't treat her right.

And Jaxson very much wanted to be that better man.

He glanced at his phone—a quarter past one. He'd give her one more call, but if she didn't pick up, he was going to her apartment and banging on the door until she let him in. This time, the phone didn't even ring... it just went straight to message. Which meant she had turned it off.

Dammit.

That's it—he was going over there to talk to her. He grabbed his keys and headed toward the door of his office, only to see Jace dashing around the common room and peering into the offices.

"Jace?" Jaxson stopped at the threshold of his office. He hadn't seen his brother since he had cleared out the Wilding pack, hopefully taking them to the safehouse outside the city. "What's up?"

"Hey," Jace said, a little breathless as he jogged up to Jaxson. "Have you seen Jared?"

"Nope. Just me in the office this morning."

Jace gave him a cockeyed look. "Why are you even here, bro? I thought you'd be spending the weekend in bed with a certain hot office assistant."

"That's... got some complications." Jaxson grimaced. "I'm on my way to see her now, actually."

Jace shook his head. "Man, why are you even messing around with her? I mean, I did what you said and stashed Terra at the safehouse, but she is *so ready* for a mate. It was all I could do to keep her from climbing into my bed last night."

"At the *safehouse?*" Jaxson's eyebrows hiked up. The safehouse was their family estate in the mountains outside Seattle, and their *mother* was the caretaker.

"I know, right?" Jace looked disgusted. "Mom would've stirred up a shitstorm if she knew. Now, if it was *you* bedding Terra, I think Mom would have made you two breakfast and started planning the wedding." He smirked.

Jaxson rolled his eyes. Their mother wasn't just on the bandwagon to find him a mate—she was driving the wagon train. The estate had been a halfway house for all kinds of shifters ever since Dad died, so she was probably used to a few bed-shakings in the middle of the night. It wasn't like his mother didn't know the passionate nature of wolves and other shifters. But only a Wilding would try to seduce one of her sons while under her roof.

"Thanks for running interference on that for me," Jaxson said, still grimacing. "So what's up with Jared? I thought he'd already taken off for the mountains for the weekend."

Jace frowned. "I thought he had—but he must have found reception last night because he eventually returned my call about the mission to rescue Cassie. I told him all about it and the warehouse and everything. He was *pissed* that he'd missed out." Jace huffed a small laugh and shook his head.

"I'll bet." Of the three of them, Jared was the most intent on direct assaults from the beginning. Only problem being that they didn't know where to point the assault team. "So is he coming in?" Jaxson asked, glancing around at the darkened offices.

"That's just it. I thought he was coming to the safehouse. We were all tired, so we crashed pretty much right away. When I woke up, he still hadn't showed. I've been calling, but he hasn't been picking up. I thought maybe he'd come here…" Jace's voice drifted off as his eyes went wide.

Jaxson figured it out at the same time. "He went after the warehouse."

"*Shit.*" Jace grimaced. "Oh *man,* I shouldn't have told him."

"It's not your fault, Jace." Jaxson rubbed his hand across the stubble on his face. "But if he's not answering his phone…"

"Shit, shit, *shit.* He's in there, isn't he? They got him." Jace took his frustration out on the door frame, leaving a small dent.

"Hey!" Jaxson gave him a glare. "It's all right. We'll get him out."

"What if they move him? What if he's not even

there?" Jace was running a rough hand through his hair. "If I'd been infiltrated, I'd decamp right away."

"Right. Which is why Jared went after them, I'm sure. Because he didn't want them slithering off into the night." Damn, this was a mess. "All right, did Murphy go to the safehouse last night or did he go home?"

"I just took the Wildings to the safehouse. Everyone else went home."

"Murphy lives closest to the edge of town where the warehouse is," Jaxson said. "We need eyes on that immediately. Get that in place, then round up a team. Maybe ten. If we've got surveillance, they can't decamp without us knowing. And if they're still inside, we might have to wait until dark to move in."

"Understood." Jace already had his phone out, dialing Murphy.

"I need to make a stop at Olivia's," Jaxson said. "I'll meet you there."

Jace held up his hands in a questioning way, but Murphy must have picked up because he turned away and took the call. Jaxson left his unspoken question unanswered and jogged out of the office, heading for his car. He needed to make sure Olivia was all right before he dove into a mission he knew he might not come back from.

He had to pound on Olivia's door ten times before she finally opened.

"Jaxson, for God's sake—" she said, but he just brushed past her and stepped into the apartment.

He peered around before saying anything. If *asshole boyfriend* was here, he would take care of that first. But the place was clear.

"Sure, come on in," she said with heavy sarcasm. But she closed the door behind her. "Please, barge into my apartment, even though I distinctly told you to stay the hell away."

He cocked his head. "You did *not* tell me stay away. You merely said you had an asshole for a boyfriend."

She folded her arms. "I did *not* say he was an asshole."

He shrugged one shoulder. "Details."

She shook her head, like she couldn't believe his audacity, but he could tell she'd been crying. *A lot.* Before he even thought about what he was doing, he had her backed up against the door, hands on either side of her head. He wasn't actually touching her, but he was ready to kiss those tears away.

Her eyes were wide.

"Any man who doesn't see how wonderful you are is a

complete idiot," he said softly. He wasn't going to trot out his strong suspicion that this millionaire boyfriend didn't even exist... not until he knew the real reason why she was pushing him away.

"Yeah, well, maybe I'm one of those girls who likes unavailable men." She was saying it defiantly, straight into his face, but she wasn't trying to push him back or move away. Her words were shoving him away, but her trembling lips and heaving chest were saying something entirely different.

"What's his name, Olivia?" he said with a little more edge in his voice. "I'd like to have a word with him."

Her eyes were glassing over again. "Jaxson, *please*. Just leave it alone!"

He frowned. That plea was real—he could feel it. She was truly afraid of something.

"I don't know what hold this man has over you, but I'm not giving up without a fight." Then he leaned in, almost close enough to kiss, but stopping short of actually touching his lips to hers. "You're worth fighting for," he whispered against her lips. Then he did kiss her, pressing her luscious body up against the door as he tasted her sweet mouth. She responded to him, just as she had last night, allowing him into her mouth even as her hands gripped his shoulders hard. She seemed unable to decide whether to pull him closer or push him away.

He broke the kiss, but her electric touch brought back every rush of pleasure from the night before. His body ached for more, but he couldn't stay.

"You care about me. I know you do," he whispered in her ear. "And I want to be the man you finally let into your life." Then he pulled back to look into her eyes.

Her tears were gone, and she was blinking, rapidly, stunned by something—either the kiss or his words, he didn't know which. But that was all he had to give right now. He had to make sure his brother wasn't being taken apart by whoever had captured him.

"I'm sorry, I have to go now," he said, easing back and breaking the close personal space they were in. "Jared's in trouble."

A frown crashed through her stunned expression. "What? What happened?"

"I think he's gone after the people who kidnaped Cassie. We found a warehouse where they might be keeping the others. Jared's an ex-Marine sharpshooter, tough as all hell, but if he went in there alone, I don't know what he was thinking. He's not always…" He hesitated. Olivia didn't need to know all the crazy that went on with the River brothers.

"Not always concerned for his own life?" Olivia's frown grew deeper. "There's a dark side to him, isn't there?"

JAXSON

"Yes." But Jaxson was relieved. He should have known she would understand. "And while I'm sure he has the best of intentions, I don't trust him not to go blazing into a situation he won't actually live through."

"So you're going after him." The selfless concern on her face made Jaxson's heart ache.

He wanted nothing more than to come back and make this woman his own… if he could only convince her to let him. "Yes. Jace is gathering a team. We're watching the warehouse to make sure they don't move anyone, but we might not go in until nightfall."

She nodded. Then she pursed her lips, uncertain about something. Suddenly, she threw her arms around him and hugged him tight. "Be careful," she whispered.

He held her close, relishing every bit of her concern and every second of her body pressed against his. Then he loosened his hold and kissed her again. This time she didn't hold back, and it nearly made him groan with the need to have her. *Again.* Always.

When he finally broke the kiss, he said, breathless, "I'm coming back for you." His voice was rough with too much emotion. He had no experience with goodbyes—he had never let himself care about someone enough to have to say one that mattered. He ducked his head so she wouldn't see the emotion betrayed across it.

Then he strode out the door.

CHAPTER 14

Olivia leaned against the closed door of her apartment, breathless.

Breathless from the goodbye Jaxson had just given her. Breathless from his kiss and his words and everything he was and did. *You're worth fighting for.* It brought tears to her eyes, but it also made her heart pound with fear. Because the words inked on his chest might as well be etched in his soul—*all in, all the time.* If Jaxson River decided to fight for something, he wasn't going to stop until he got it.

Only that something was *her*. And he had no idea what

he was getting into.

She rubbed her eyes, clearing them of the lingering tears.

There had to be some way to stop Jaxson from wanting her. She was completely failing at that so far. The minute he opened that sexy mouth and said *anything*—much less put it on hers—she was complete putty in his hands. And her lie about loving another man wasn't any deterrent at all! It was crazy. Jaxson River could have any woman—any human female would drop her panties for him, three shifter females were lined up waiting to mate him, and even a crazed witch from his past wanted him so badly that she cursed him—and he still wanted Olivia Lilyfield, ex-reporter and current-secretary.

The only explanation was that he couldn't find a real mate. If he hadn't been cursed, Jaxson would have settled down long ago, having pups and leading his pack like the alpha wolf he was supposed to be. The alpha he *was*.

Olivia straightened up from the door as it dawned on her: *that was it*.

She could lift the curse.

All this time, she'd locked away the part of her that was a witch. And that still needed to be kept deep inside—it was too dangerous to mess with—but she had also fled all ties to the witching world after she turned her parents into dust. She wanted nothing to do with any of it. But she still had an aunt in a powerful coven... maybe her aunt could find a way to break the curse that kept Jaxson from finding his perfect mate.

A sudden clarity came to her mind: *this was what she was meant to do.*

All her life, she strove to find the thing that would redeem her, make up for what happened to her parents. If she could accomplish this—if she could free Jaxson—it would be the *one good thing* she had been looking for. The one thing she was uniquely able to do that *mattered.*

But only if her aunt would take her call—which was by no means certain.

Olivia raced to her tiny bedroom and dug through her closet. She had a box of things left over from the fire. The few treasures she kept and hauled from foster care to foster care. It was small—a box for size-two dance shoes, which was how tiny her feet were at the time, back when they had money for lessons. The fire had charred the corners, and the lid had incurred some damage over the years, but it was still intact, buried under some winter sweaters on the back of her closet shelf. She hauled it out and took it to her bed.

Her hand shook a little before opening it. She hadn't gone through it in *years.*

The contents were as meager and bedraggled as the box: a necklace of her mom's, her dad's eyeglasses with the lens broken, a dozen tiny shells from a visit to the beach not long before the fire, and... a tiny black notebook. Olivia snatched that out and closed the lid. She thumbed through it. Her mom's precise and flowery print was so pretty, even faded after all these years. Most of the names Olivia didn't know, but the one she needed was still there: *Guinevere Damon.*

Olivia's hand shook a little more as she dialed the number.

"Hello?" The rich female voice that answered seemed tentative.

"Is this Guinevere Damon?" Olivia asked.

"Depends on who's asking." Her voice had turned sultry, but Olivia could tell it was her.

"Auntie Gwen... it's your niece, Olivia."

Silence. Olivia held her breath.

Finally, there was a long exhalation of breath on the other end. "For the love of magic... Rowan's girl has come home."

This was a terrible idea. Olivia knew that.

But walking into a coven of witches was the only way to get what she needed: the magic to break Jaxson's curse. For that, she'd do just about anything. Which, apparently, included visiting her Aunt Gwen's office in downtown Seattle.

Urban Damon Design was etched on the glass entrance to the coven's graphic design company. It was one of the largest and most prestigious in the city, doing work for all the big technology companies as well as the cutting-edge start-ups. Of course, all their preternaturally beautiful designs were conjured by the witches who filled the company's ranks from top to bottom. Olivia didn't know exactly how they used magic in their work, but she doubted it was design talent alone that landed them all those big contracts.

She pushed the door open and tried to keep her chin up, even though she was a ball of nerves. Aunt Gwen was waiting for her at the front desk with a smile that reminded Olivia far too much of her mother's.

She didn't expect that particular heartache. It made her low-heeled shoes catch on the luxurious white carpeting just inside the door. Her aunt hurried to her side and looked like she wanted to hug Olivia... which just made her stumble back to keep out of reach.

It was both terrifying and tremendously awkward. She grimaced.

Her aunt looked pained, but pulled her hands back and clasped them together. "My dear Olivia, you cannot even imagine how happy I am that you've returned to us."

JAXSON

"I, um…" Olivia straightened her blouse. "I'm not exactly staying, Aunt Gwen. But thanks for meeting me on such short notice."

She'd put on her best office attire for this, but her overly curvy body and plain blouse and skirt were vastly outclassed by her aunt, whose trim form was elegantly encased in a perfectly tailored red suit. Her nails were like small daggers and likewise fire-engine red. All of it set off a beautiful mane of black hair that tumbled in waves down to her waist. Her aunt was *super-model gorgeous*—more than any female shifter Olivia had ever seen—and it was clear that Olivia inherited her father's genes in the looks department. Either that, or Aunt Gwen was using magic to enhance her beauty, like Jaxson suggested. She was ostensibly Olivia's mother's age, but she didn't look a day over thirty.

"There's nothing that could have stopped me from meeting with you, dear." Gwen seemed to really mean it. "I'm just so relieved you've finally reached out to me. I thought for sure you would never… well… *embrace* your heritage."

"I'm not a witch," Olivia said hastily. *Too hastily.* And it sounded pretty defensive. "I mean, I'm not a practicing witch. Because… well…"

"It's because of the fire, dear. I know." Her aunt's lovely face drew down in what looked like genuine compassion. Olivia didn't know her at all, not really, but that single look and those words... she couldn't keep the tears from welling up in her eyes.

"Oh, you poor, poor thing. Going through all of that alone. And with no one to guide you in your magical development." She looked like she wanted to hug Olivia again, but Olivia knew all too well that a witch's touch was her most potent weapon.

She folded up her arms to dissuade Aunt Gwen from any such ideas. "I wouldn't have bothered you, Aunt Gwen, but I need your help. With a spell."

"A spell?" Her perfectly-shaped eyebrows lifted. "Indeed. Sounds like something we should discuss in my office." She ushered Olivia past the receptionist's desk, down the hall, and into an exquisitely decorated office that looked out over the bay. The furniture was all burnished dark woods, and an entire wall was lined with bookcases, only instead of books, there were dozens of jeweled containers in every shape and size.

Once the door was closed, Gwen said, "Whatever you need, dear, I'm sure we can take care of it. Are you in some kind of trouble?"

"Not exactly." Olivia frowned. She hadn't really given thought to how to phrase this. "I need to break a curse." That seemed like a good place to start.

Gwen's green eyes flashed. "Has someone put a curse

on you, Livvy?" It was her nickname from when she was just a child, and it speared Olivia with memories that tore into her heart.

She cleared her throat. "No, I promise. This is for a friend. Another witch put a curse on him, and I need to break it."

The fiery anger went out of her aunt's eyes. "Well, I'm glad to hear it's not you, dear. I'm afraid I might have had some serious issues with a witch who dared to curse my niece."

A warm feeling flooded Olivia's chest, threatening to bring back the tears. No one had looked out for her in a long time. Except Jaxson, but that was different. Gwen might be a witch, but she was treating Olivia like she was really *family*.

Olivia gave her a small smile. "That's really sweet of you, Aunt Gwen."

This lit up her aunt's face. All smiles, she edged a little closer to Olivia, obviously holding herself back from another embrace. "We tend to be very protective of our own, Miss Olivia." Then she rubbed her hands together with mock glee. "Now tell me what spell we can do to help out your poor, little cursed friend. It's not every day I get to do magic with my niece."

Olivia shrugged. "I don't know what spell would work, precisely. And my friend isn't exactly *little*... but he's been cursed so that he can never take a mate."

Gwen's smile evaporated. "A mate. You mean, he's a shifter. A wolf to be precise."

Olivia bit her lip. "Yeah. A witch wanted him, and when he said no…"

"She denied him the pleasure of a mate." Gwen rolled her eyes. "I love my coven sisters, but I swear, some of them can be *so* dramatic."

Olivia grimaced. It hadn't occurred to her that the witch who cursed Jaxson might be in her family's coven… or a distant relative. It wasn't like there were millions of witches populating Seattle. The covens were small and generally knew each other. Although Olivia got the sense that they kept their distance.

"Why do you have such an interest in this wolf?" The fire was back in Gwen's eyes. "Please tell me you're not tangled up with him. They're sexual beasts but really not good for much else."

Olivia straightened. "Jaxson is a good man."

Her face transformed into a picture of horror, briefly, then melted into a piteous expression. "Oh, dear. You're in love with the creature."

Olivia scowled at her aunt's obvious lack of respect for wolves, but there wasn't much use in denying it. "Yes."

She nodded. "And you want him for your own."

JAXSON

"No." Olivia glared at her aunt, daring her to question it.

She frowned. "I don't quite—"

Olivia balled up her fists. "Jaxson needs to be free to choose his own mate. A proper mate. And I'm his only chance to make that happen. This is *my* only chance to do something decent with my life for once. To make up for—"

Gwen's eyes had gone wide.

"To make up for killing my parents." All the air went out of Olivia's lungs. She said it. Finally. *Out loud.* And to the one person who could destroy her by barely lifting a finger.

Gwen's face twisted up. "Olivia, dear, that wasn't your fault! You were just a child, coming into your powers and—"

Olivia held up her hand to cut her off. She'd made all the excuses in her own head for years. None of it changed the fact that her parents were dead by her own hand. "It doesn't matter. It happened. And I can't undo it. What matters *now* is that I need to break this curse. Before I'm too in love with Jaxson to be able to let him go." She was afraid it might already be too late for that, but she was going to *try*.

Gwen's concern wrinkled up her magically young face… then slowly, it relaxed. She was silent for a moment, seeming to look all over the air surrounding Olivia. She remembered that scanning look from when she was a child, when her mother would read her aura. Her aunt was judging her somehow by the essence of her intentions. Her thoughts. Olivia kept still and quiet while she did, hoping that she'd see Olivia's determination in the colors visible only to true witches.

Finally, her aunt nodded. "I see. Well, then. We better find a way to break this spell."

Olivia's body sagged with relief. Then, impulsively, she reached out and threw her arms around the tall, gorgeous witch who was going to save not only Jaxson, but her as well. "Thank you so much, Aunt Gwen."

When she pulled back, there was a shine in Gwen's eyes to go with her smile.

Chapter 15

Jaxson pulled his car up to the meeting spot where Jace had assembled the assault team.

Everyone, including Jaxson, had changed into combat gear—lightweight body armor they could still shift out of, if necessary, plus ultra-light helmets with built-in mics for communicating while human. All told, they had two vans, one car, a dozen shifters, and a small arsenal of weapons and tech for taking down the gate. The meetup was two blocks away from the warehouse, and the sun was starting to sink, but the cover of night was still hours away.

"What's our status?" Jaxson asked his brother, who was holding one of their secure handsets to his ear.

Jace held up a finger, listened to something on the handset. "Copy that." Then he turned to Jaxson. "About half an hour ago, a van arrived and entered the gate. It drove straight into the warehouse through a back garage door. Nothing has left since Murphy arrived and set up his surveillance, and there's obviously still activity on the ground, so…"

Jaxson nodded. "You think Jared's still in there." The bad guys wouldn't bring new shifter victims to the warehouse, if they'd already decamped from that location. "What do you think they're waiting for?"

Jace shrugged. "Maybe they think Jared is the extent of our plans for assault?"

Jaxson frowned. That seemed unlikely. "More likely they don't have a good place to go. Biding their time until they get a new prison set up."

Jace nodded his agreement. "Either way, *someone* is still there. And I'm betting Jared is, too."

"Agreed." Jaxson glanced at the late-afternoon sun. "Time is still against us. I don't think we can wait until nightfall."

"I thought you might say that." Jace smirked and waved over Taylor. He brought a handful of gear—thick rubber gloves, a long metal rod, and jumper cables. No doubt his electrical-fence-breaking kit.

"Hey, boss," Taylor said. "I'm ready to take 'er down whenever you say."

Jaxson looked askance at the equipment. "We're not going to have much surprise on our side. Which means we need overwhelming force. Shock and awe."

Jace cocked his head. "What are you thinking? Just ramming the gate?"

"We're going to have to do that regardless," Jaxson said. "Cutting through the fence and going on foot is too slow. Too much time for them to react. On the other hand, the distance between the road and the shack is pretty small. They won't see the truck coming until we're breathing down their necks."

Taylor looked disappointed.

"However, I'm worried about shocking the vehicles and dragging a ton of electrified razor wire with us into the compound." He tipped his head to Taylor. "So I still want you to blow the fence, but I need you to wait until we're about to ram. That means you're sitting this one out, Taylor. And watching our rear flank."

Taylor nodded. "You got it, boss." He flicked on his headset and spoke through the mic. "I'll be set up in ten." Then he trotted off with his gear toward the warehouse.

Jace winced as he watched Taylor go. "I wish we had

more manpower on this."

Jaxson glanced at the crew they had remaining. He and Jace were ex-military—Jace was an Army medic, but he'd seen more than his share of combat—and all rest of the Riverwise pack had military experience of one kind or another.

There was one shifter he didn't recognize mixing in with his crew.

"Who's the grunt?" Jaxson asked, gesturing with his chin to the dark-haired kid chatting it up with Murphy. He was young, probably no more than twenty-two.

"Daniel Wilding. He's Army, active duty, stateside between tours. Son of a lieutenant colonel in the Wilding pack. After what went down with Cassie, he wanted in on anything we were planning."

Jaxson nodded. "All right. Brief everyone on the plan. We'll head out as soon as Taylor gives the go."

Jace gave a quick nod and jogged off toward the group of shifters gathered around the vans. Jaxson knew they had all tallied up the odds when they signed up for this, but he still didn't like it. They hadn't tried a direct assault from the beginning due to lack of intel… but also because it was dangerous, and it tipped their hand, exposing who they were and endangering the entire pack. But more importantly, they still didn't know who they were up against.

And an unknown enemy was the most dangerous kind.

But they didn't have a choice at this point. He wasn't going to leave Jared to rot in their cells, enduring whatever went on in that warehouse. His brother had already been through too much—more than any man or shifter should have to. Jaxson wasn't going to let them slice into him any further, physically or mentally.

They piled into the vans and waited for Taylor's signal. When it came, they formed a two-van caravan, gaining speed until they took the turn toward the gate. Jaxson drove the lead van with Jace riding shotgun. Jace gave the thumbs up that Taylor had blown the fence just before they reached the shack. The surprised guard couldn't get off a shot before they crashed the gate, but gunfire quickly followed after.

Jaxson sped around the back of the warehouse, gaining cover behind the square aluminum-siding building and also seeking out the rear garage door. Dust clouded around the van as he skidded to a stop. The second van was right beside him. His shifters spilled out of both vehicles and sprinted toward the building, taking up stations, weapons at the ready, on either side of the garage door. A small human-sized door to the side was an ambush waiting to happen, and they didn't have time for Murphy and his munitions to blow the garage door. It looked flimsy enough, and he hoped like hell it would give way to the van, because that was all they had for a battering ram. He threw it in reverse to gain some distance, slammed to another stop, then gunned the engine and popped the clutch, spinning out rocks behind the van as it barreled toward the door.

He ducked behind the cover of the dashboard just before impact.

The shock threw him against the seat then knocked him hard on the van's oversized steering wheel, but the van kept going, so he blindly jammed his foot on the brake. The van skidded to a stop. His vision was doubled for a moment, and he couldn't see into the murk inside the warehouse anyway, but he heard the shouts of his crew as they spilled into the building after him. He blinked away the blurriness and checked the side mirror, which was shockingly intact—they had definitely breached the door, which was a blown-out wreckage of sheet metal behind him. The van was still running. He tensed to use it as a weapon if there were forces inside the warehouse... but as far as he could tell with the dusty, dim light, it was empty.

Jaxson blinked, put the van into park, and climbed out.

His crew were likewise standing in the middle of the warehouse with wary but amazed looks on their faces.

JAXSON

The place was two stories tall, with darkened rafters filling the upper half, but it was the ground level that attracted their attention. Steel-barred cages, ten by ten, stood empty except for mangy cots and what looked like buckets for toilets.

"There's the van," Jace said over his helmet mic. He was at the front of their crew, pointing to a white van at the far end.

"So where's the driver?" Jaxson replied, pulling his weapon out and sweeping along the empty cages. But he couldn't see anyone in the entire building. As he crept forward with the rest of the crew, checking each cell, he heard a muffled grunt.

Jaxson said over the mic, "Everyone hold."

They stilled and listened. The muffled sound came again, with some rattling this time.

"It's coming from the van," Jace said, hurrying forward. His men were already on it. As they got closer, a medical station was revealed behind it. Cabinets and tables and gleaming metal instrumentation that was obviously used for some kind of medical procedure on the inmates. Jaxson picked up his pace, but just as a shining silver table swung into view, and he saw *someone strapped to it* with hand and foot restraints, he heard one of his crew shout, "It's Jared!"

Jaxson screeched to a stop as dread washed through

him. "Jace!" he shouted.

But it was too late.

A popping, like firecrackers, filled the warehouse—Jaxson recognized the sound of tranquilizer darts just as his men started dropping like flies. Jaxson swung his weapon around wildly, looking for the source, realizing too late the ambush came from above. He fired off several rounds at the shadowy figures filling the rafters, but darts pinched his shoulder, legs, and chest simultaneously. A half dozen bee bites that blurred his vision and clattered his gun to the floor.

He shifted to wolf form, dislodging the darts and leaving them behind with his clothing, but his paws scrabbled ineffectively on the concrete floor. The tranq was already turning his limbs useless, even in wolf form.

A trap. The whole thing was a trap.

Jaxson only got a few feet toward his fallen brothers before the darkness took him.

CHAPTER 16

"Why do I have to be involved?" Olivia asked.

Aunt Gwen pursed her perfectly shaped lips. "Well, we could invite your shifter friend *here* to help us determine whether the curse is still in effect. But that probably wouldn't end well."

No, it wouldn't. Plus Olivia didn't want Jaxson to know anything about this until it was complete... and irreversible. "All right," she said with a sigh. "What do I have to do?"

"I need some essence of the man, something to help me find him in the magical world."

Olivia frowned, suddenly uncertain. "You're not going to *do* anything to him... are you?"

"Well, of course not, dear." Gwen's face twisted up like Olivia had suggested she take a dip in the dumpster outside the coven's high-rise office.

"It's just that... I *know* shifters and witches are mortal enemies." Olivia bit her lip, hoping she wasn't crossing a line here.

"Unless we're in bed together." Gwen's face transformed from horrified into a smirk in no time flat.

"And maybe even then," Olivia countered. "I've heard the stories, Aunt Gwen."

She just rolled her eyes. "Do you believe every story you hear about shifters?"

A fair point. "All right," she conceded. "Back to the spell—what kind of essence of Jaxson do you need?"

"A memory. The more intimate, the better."

Olivia scrunched up her nose. Sharing that just seemed... wrong.

"Well, it would be easier with a hair sample or article of clothing, but I'm assuming you didn't bring any of that."

Olivia sighed. "No."

Gwen strode over to one of the burnished-wood bookcases that lined her office and plucked a pinch of something out of an iridescent glass box. She brought it back to Olivia and sifted the whitish powder with the fingers of one hand, letting it fall into the palm of the other.

"Would you like to learn how to do a seeking spell, Miss Olivia?" Aunt Gwen's eyes were lit up with delight.

"I'm not doing any magic, Aunt Gwen." Olivia scowled.

The delight faded. "My dear, you're going to have to learn someday."

"No, really, I don't." When Gwen looked unconvinced, Olivia added, "I mean it, Aunt Gwen. I'm not going there."

"Very well." Her lips pursed again and waved her hand over the tiny pile of white dust, whispering some kind of incantation. The words must have been from another language because Olivia couldn't understand them. Returning to English, her aunt said, "You'll only be a bystander in this one—providing a key ingredient for the spell, if you will. I'll be doing all the magic."

Olivia nodded her consent.

The dust in her aunt's hand began to smoke, and a swirl of tiny blue sparks dove through the small cloud in her hand. Gwen held her hand up to Olivia's face, and then gently blew the smoke her way.

Olivia did expect *that*, but her gasp only sucked the smoke directly into her lungs. She huffed it out again, thinking she might cough, but instead the world just got a little blurry around the edges. Her aunt's face loomed large nearby.

"Think about a time you were intimate with Jaxson." Her voice seemed to boom too loudly, like they were suddenly in an immense room, and her aunt had grown ten times her original size. The office walls warped in the periphery of Olivia's vision. "Find a time when he touched your very soul."

Images of Jaxson flashed before Olivia's eyes—his smile, his deep chuckle, their lovemaking—but the image that zoomed up and stayed was him leaning close to her, forcing her back against the door of her apartment and whispering, *You're worth fighting for.*

"Oh my," Aunt Gwen breathed in appreciation. "I can see why you're fond of that one."

That made the image wobble a little, and hot embarrassment shot through Olivia, but she grabbed hold of the memory—it was also the reason she was trying so hard to lift his curse. Without it, Jaxson wouldn't fight so hard and come so dangerously close to her.

The image was frozen before her now, and the blue sparks from the spell cloud swirled around his body, buzzing like bees looking for a place to land.

"The magic is strong with this one," Gwen

murmured. "His own, as well as another's."

The vision vanished, returning Olivia to the plain, reality-filled sight of the office. It was jarring to her mind, making her teeter for a moment.

She blinked away the vertigo. "Well? Did you get what you needed?"

Gwen's lips were turned down. "I'm afraid the spell is still tightly bound to him."

"How can we break it?"

"We can't, dear," Gwen said with a sigh. "Only the one who cast it can break it. Alternatively, we could let the spell fulfill its original purpose. Then it will dissipate of its own accord."

"It's purpose was to kill Jaxson's mate!" She could hardly believe her aunt would suggest that as an option.

"I agree it's an unfortunate turn for that particular female," she mused. "On the upside, he would be free to mate again." She waggled her eyebrows.

"Gwen!" Olivia's mouth dropped open.

Her aunt shrugged like it was no big deal. "It was just a thought."

Olivia's shoulders slumped. "There has to be another way." She turned away from her aunt, still horrified by what she suggested, and pretended to study the multitude of glass jars and boxes on her shelf. What other awful things had her aunt contemplated doing, much less carried out, with all these powders and the incantations that went with them? Jaxson was right to believe that witches were basically evil... and not just the one who cursed him. Although that witch definitely took it to a twisted level. How selfish would you have to be to deny someone a chance at true love simply because he wouldn't please you in bed? Not that Jaxson's pleasuring-abilities weren't epic, but still.

Then it clicked... Olivia turned back to her aunt. "You said the witch who cast the spell could break it."

Gwen's face twisted up in disbelief. "Well, the moon could fall out of the sky tomorrow... but it's highly unlikely to do so."

Olivia strode back to her. "You know who she is."

"Yes," Gwen said emphatically. "And I know the last thing on earth she would consider is revoking a spell of this kind."

"Maybe I can persuade her."

"You?" Gwen shook her head, eyes wide. "Olivia, my dear, you're not even a fledgling witch. You shy away from the smallest of spells. Sybil would eat you alive."

"You could help me." Olivia edged closer. *"Please,* Aunt Gwen."

"Oh, for the love of magic." Her aunt gave her a look like her long-lost niece might be more trouble than she was worth.

Olivia rushed out. "I'll do anything, Aunt Gwen. I'll… I'll even try some magic. Maybe. Nothing too crazy. Only because it's dangerous. *I'm* dangerous."

Her aunt's green eyes softened. "You're not *dangerous*, dear. You're just… *inexperienced*. And you come from a very powerful line of witches. With the right training, you could become an amazing asset to our coven."

"I… I *would* like to learn how to control it." *That* was a complete lie. Joining a coven of witches was the last thing on earth she would ever do. But she could backtrack on her promise later. Or think of something. "Do this for me, Auntie Gwen, and I promise, I'll give it a try."

"It's been my dream all these years to have you join us, Olivia, but… you have to understand. Sybil is very unlikely to grant your request. Even with my… *persuasion*." Her aunt's face pinched up with worry.

But Olivia already knew all that. And she was sure this witch, Sybil, was dangerous as well. "I have to try."

Gwen sighed. "All right." Then she wagged a finger at Olivia. "But let me do the talking. Sybil isn't someone you want to cross."

Then she twirled in her perfect red suit and lead Olivia out the door.

"Is this some kind of crass little joke?" Sybil's disgust

was palpable.

Aunt Gwen stood tall under the other witch's glare.

Olivia lurked behind her aunt's thin frame.

Sybil wasn't part of her mother's coven—in fact, she didn't have a coven at all. As far as Olivia could tell, Sybil was flying solo in her one-woman consulting firm not far from *Urban Damon Design's* office. Maybe even fellow witches couldn't stand her? She was as beautiful as Jaxson claimed—mile-high cheekbones, long raven hair, porcelain skin—but it was a haughty kind of beauty, with eyes as cold and black as space. Her barely-there, cleavage-baring purple silk blouse clung to her ample breasts and draped over her pencil-thin black skirt, amping up the sex appeal. A small trail of smoke curled menacingly from the thin finger she had pointed at Gwen.

"This isn't a joke, Sybil," her aunt said evenly. "And in exchange for this small favor, I'm sure *Urban Damon* could toss a few clients your way."

"I don't need your clients!" Sybil's voice deepened like a storm gathering power.

Olivia glanced around the office—the furnishings were all extremely high end, but that could easily be glamour. The office itself was in an older, somewhat shabby high-rise, right on the edge of downtown where it started to transition to the area with the homeless shelter.

Sybil certainly wasn't doing as well as *Urban Damon,* no matter what she claimed.

"What's your price, then, Sybil?" Gwen's voice was still even, but Olivia could tell she was already starting to lose patience. "Surely there's something we can work out with this."

"Why do you care what happens to this shifter, anyway?" Sybil peered around Gwen to cast a bone-chilling look upon Olivia. "And who is this fledging you have hiding in your skirts?"

"She's my niece." The friendliness of Gwen's voice dropped two levels. "She's in training. I simply brought her along to observe."

"Training?" Sybil wrinkled her nose up in disgust. "Rather old for that. A little slow, is she?"

Gwen's hands flexed, and a bit of smoke leaked from them as well, but she kept them at her sides.

Sybil huffed her disdain for Olivia and turned back to Gwen. "So why all the interest in pretty little Jaxson? I suppose he's all grown up now. And probably twice as hot. Hmm… on second thought, why don't you tell me where he is? I'd be happy to make a deal with *him.*"

Olivia's heart lurched. *No, no, no.*

But Gwen's back stiffened. "The shifter is under my protection, Sybil Domina LeCroix. If you touch a hair on his head, you'll be answering to *me.* And all the sisters of the Damon coven."

"Ooooh, I see." Sybil drew the words out. "Is that how it is? Have you developed a taste for wolf now, Guinevere?" She smirked, and it turned Olivia's stomach. "Well, then, you can have the little heart-breaker… if you can handle him. All you have to do is let him sink those sexy fangs into you, dearie."

"I'm not stupid, Sybil." Gwen's voice was ice cold. "I can read a curse. You've poisoned his bite."

"Well, *yes*… his bite is certain to kill a mere *shifter*." Sybil's smirk grew even more menacing. "But you're such a *powerful* witch, Guinevere Damon, I'm sure you could counter that magical poison easily enough."

Olivia's eyes went wide. *Was that true?*

Gwen glared at Sybil. "You're lying."

Sybil fanned her fingers around her head. "Am I? Read my aura and tell me I'm leading a sister witch astray." Her voice was purring, and it certainly *sounded* like a cagey lie.

But Olivia couldn't read her aura at all.

Gwen was staring hard at the air around Sybil's head. "You're saying I could take the bite and survive?"

Sybil's evil smile grew. "I'm saying, if you're *truly* a powerful witch, Gwen dearie, you'd have a fair shot at fighting it off. The curse is only as strong as I am, after all. And you and your sisters in the Damon coven are all *so* much more powerful than little old me." Her smirk settled into a cold challenge. "If you want the wolf... *take him*. And then we'll see who's the stronger witch."

Gwen's hand flexed and ball of blue energy swirled in it. "It's truly a wonder no one's yet turned you to ash, Sybil."

She fluttered her thin fingers. "Kiss-kiss to you, too, Guinevere." She dropped her voice. "Now get out of my office."

Gwen gave her one last glare before turning on her heel and striding out of the tiny, one-room office. Olivia hurried after her, half expecting to get a bolt of witch magic in her back as she fled.

Once they were safely in the elevator, heading to the bottom floor, Olivia asked, "Was she telling the truth? Could a powerful enough witch take the bite and survive?"

"She was telling the truth," Gwen said through her teeth. "But that's not the kind of risk most witches are going to sign up for. *Especially* for a shifter."

"Maybe not *most* witches," Olivia said quietly.

Gwen slowly turned to her, eyes wide. "Do not... *no!* Olivia, you can't even think about doing something like that!"

But Olivia *was* thinking about it. Even more, a plan was already forming in her mind.

Chapter 17

Jaxson felt the bindings around his wrists before anything else.

Awareness slowly faded in, but he kept his eyes closed, and his body inert. He wanted to jerk up from where he was sitting—some kind of hard surface was under him, probably a chair, hands bound together in front—but he knew better than that. This was his chance to evaluate his situation and remember how he got here before his captor knew he was—

A hard smack across the face whipped his head to the side.

JAXSON

Jaxson blinked his eyes open and turned to glare at whoever had just hit him.

"I juiced you with a stimulant, *Jaxson River*. Don't play possum with me." The man standing before him was mid-thirties, dark suit, clunky not tailored, lean-muscled body, and weasely eyes. *Government,* for sure. Too soft for military, possibly intelligence.

So, they'd been caught. At least Jaxson was moving up the food chain.

He straightened in the chair, subtly testing his restraints. Hands bound with zip ties in front of him. Legs bound as well, one to each leg of the chair. "I'm sorry, have we met?" Jaxson asked conversationally.

"I'm *shocked* you don't remember me," the man said with a smirk.

Jaxson pulled a fake scowl... but then it clicked. He was one of the men from the alleyway. The ones with the cattle prods. "Ah, yes, the one who brought the toys. Good times, Agent...?"

"You can call me Agent Smith." *Agent Smith* chuckled at his own joke.

Jaxson shook his head, supposedly at the awful humor, but he was really using the opportunity to scan his surroundings. His men were bound and unconscious on the ground behind him. Several paramilitary types, probably hired muscle, were stationed around them, armed with holstered pistols. Jaxson couldn't get a solid count in that short of a sweep, but there were maybe a dozen guards and more shifters than Jaxson had brought with him. Which meant civilians—they must be some of the original prisoners Smith had captured.

Jaxson peered up at the government thug in front of him. "You're *adorable,* truly, Agent Smith." He lifted his bound hands. "But you should know I'm not really into the bondage thing." Then he focused inward, calling to his wolf. He could easily shift out of the zip ties, then take Smith as a hostage. He'd force the release of his pack and the other prisoners, then escape with whatever transport had brought them here. Only... his wolf was... *absent?*

That must have shown on his face because Agent Smith's chuckle grew deeper. "A little surprised are you, River? Not so easy being *just* a man, is it?"

Shit, shit, shit. A cold flush of fear trickled through Jaxson's stomach. He turned it into a smile. "I know you're still working on that *being a man* part, Agent Smith, so I won't judge." Jaxson focused harder, summoning his inner wolf with everything he had, but somehow Smith had disabled his shifting ability—all Jaxson could sense was a distant whimper, muffled, as if his wolf was bound up just like his wrists. But that stirred the magic in his blood, and a whisper of thoughts brushed his mind. At first, he thought the guards were talking behind him, but then he realized… *it was his pack.*

The humor dropped off Agent Smith's face. "As fun as this is, let's get down to business." He pounded a fist into Jaxson's face that whipped his head back against the chair. It seriously jarred Jaxson's focus… which was surely the intent.

He tasted blood in his mouth, which he took a moment to spit out and then glared at Smith. Jaxson had to keep the asshole talking while he sorted this out. "I should have realized you were into the rougher stuff, Agent Smith." At the same time, he reached out with his mind to his pack. Were they rousing from the sedative enough to help?

Smith grinned. "I'll admit, it was a pleasure to see you squirm on the ground like a dog, River. I would have enjoyed it even more had I known who you were at the time. We'll have to reprise that little bit of fun. Soon. I'll save it for when we've run out of real work to do on you."

"Can't wait." Jaxson gave Smith a bloody-mouthed smile, just to keep him off balance.

Murmurs from the pack's thoughts washed over Jaxson's mind. *Stay down! Stay down!* he broadcast to them. He was their alpha, so the command would automatically carry magical weight—a direct order was almost impossible to disobey—but most of them already knew to play possum until they had a plan.

Their responses echoed back.

Aye, aye, Captain!

Here, boss.

Yes, sir.

Jaxson... that last one was Jared. Their brother, Jace, wouldn't be able to communicate, even if he was awake, but with Jared at the ready... *All I need is a gun, brother.* Jared's thoughts rang clear in his mind. His brother was a sharpshooter in the Marines, but he had shifter-fast reflexes and deadly aim at every distance.

I'm on it. That was Daniel from the Wilding pack. *Need a little time.*

Time was something Jaxson could buy them. He peered up at the government thug still smirking down at him. "What exactly is it you want, Agent Smith?"

"I'd like to know *exactly* where you've stashed the Wilding kid. And the rest of her pack. I had special plans for her." Agent Smith's grin was too much.

Jaxson growled deep in his chest. It took everything he had to resist lunging at Smith. His pack was keeping quiet on the outside, but their mental growls were so loud they almost crowded out Smith's next words.

"Aww... you've got a soft spot for her." Smith leaned forward, hands on knees, grinning in Jaxson's face.

JAXSON

"Nice. I'll have to use that at some point."

"I'm really going to enjoy watching you die," Jaxson ground out.

Smith laughed and straightened up. "Big talk for a man tied to a chair. And a shifter unable to shift. You're clearly incompetent in the leadership department as well. You've already delivered most of your pack to me—and trust me, we'll be rounding up the others soon enough. Not much of an alpha, are you, River? And once we relocate, I'll have the truth serum pumping through you. Then you'll spill every little thing I want to know. You might as well give up the Wilding location to me now."

"How about you fuck off instead?" Jaxson held his gaze.

The corner of his mouth tipped up. "Oh, I was hoping you would say that." He hit Jaxson again, this time hard enough to screech the chair legs against the concrete floor. Jaxson took his time recovering—as if the punch actually knocked him hard enough to matter—so he could gain more situational awareness. Cavernous metal building. Smelled of gasoline. Tanks and industrial equipment lined the edges. A large garage door that constituted most of one wall was actually rolled up and open to the night air. Dark had descended while they were passed out, which was why Jaxson hadn't noticed the open door at first. Outside was a small plane, built for just a few passengers, but a substantial cargo hold. The only sounds drifting through the open hangar door were crickets, but the airplane lights were on. Was Smith planning on flying them all out? And if so, to where?

Jaxson shook his head like he was clearing it.

"Oh, come on, River," Agent Smith complained, looking disgusted. "The girl would have put up more of a fight than this."

Jaxson whipped his glare up to Smith. "What part of *fuck off* did you not understand?" he growled. *I'm losing my patience with this asshole, Daniel.* He pushed the thought out to Wilding.

This time, Smith came up from below with a punch to his jaw, then followed that with one to the right and another from the left. Jaxson let Smith beat on him without resistance, but when the last punch slipped off his face, slick with something, Jaxson had to look.

Smith was holding his hand, which was dripping with red. Could be Jaxson's blood, but the way Smith was holding it, more likely he busted his knuckles pummeling Jaxson's face.

Jaxson had to fight to repress the laugh bubbling up inside him.

Ready on your signal. Daniel's thought pinged clearly in Jaxson's head. *Murphy and I have a plan.*

Does this plan involve getting Jared a gun? Jaxson still stared at Smith's cradled hand.

Yes, sir, Daniel responded.

Wait for my move, Jaxson thought. *Then we all go. Priority is on getting Jared the weapon, then getting the prisoners out.*

Yes, sir!

Jaxson lifted his chin to point to Smith's hand. "Aww… did you hurt your hand, Agent Smith?" He used a voice so patronizing that even the smallest shifter pup would have been insulted. "Can I get you a band-aid?"

Smith gritted his teeth and came at Jaxson. Just as he reached the chair, Jaxson whipped his bound hands up to catch Smith under the chin. Then he popped up from the seat, brought his arms back down, and looped them around Smith's neck. Jaxson spun the chair still attached to his legs and dragged Smith in front of him as a human shield. Smith grabbed at his neck, struggling to breathe, but Jaxson's choke-hold was solid. And it would only take a small twist to end Smith's struggles for good.

Jaxson quickly cased the battlefield, but all hell had already broken loose.

All the shifters were up on their feet, swinging their bound wrists like clubs or taking hopping leaps at the guards with their zip-tied boots. In the melee, one of his pack had somehow found a knife, which was quickly flipping from one shifter to the next as they sliced through their zip ties. A few had their fangs out, biting their way free. Then a gun sailed through the air, from Daniel to Jared...

Hit the deck! Jaxson mentally blasted to all of his pack. Like one, they dropped to the ground... all except Jared, who Jaxson had shielded from his command. Jaxson flung himself and Agent Smith to the floor, landing with the man under him and the chair on top. Jared spun a fast circle, shooting the now-exposed guards rapid fire with dead-on aim—a couple managed to drop and scramble behind the civilian prisoners on the floor, who were just now rousing out of their sedative with the commotion.

"Hold your fire!" Jaxson shouted, but Jared had already checked his aim, pointing his gun to the ceiling to avoid hitting the prisoners. One of the guards popped up with a female shifter as a shield and started firing. Jared went down. Then Agent Smith heaved Jaxson up into the air, exposing him above the huddled masses on the floor. He caught a bullet, and it slammed him back harder than any of Agent Smith's punches. Jaxson fell backward, but his legs were still bound to the chair—that, plus the screaming pain of the gunshot wound, weakened his grip on Agent Smith. He wormed out of Jaxson's hold and twisted to slam two punches straight into Jaxson's wound. He convulsed with the pain, and black spots shot in front of his vision. By the time he blinked them clear,

JAXSON

Agent Smith was gone.

Jaxson breathed out the pain and curled up to sitting. The melee was in full force again.

Someone had taken out the guard with the gun. Shifters were engaged in hand-to-hand combat with the guards still left, which meant their weapons must be disabled or out of reach. Jaxson was hobbled by the chair, so he stayed down, casting a look around for Agent Smith. *He was running away.* The coward was making for the plane outside.

Something tugged at Jaxson's legs—he twisted to find Murphy slicing him free of the chair and then cutting his hand ties. Once out of his restraints, Jaxson sprinted toward Jared, but Jace was already there, lifting him up. Jared's shirt was covered with blood, but Jace gave Jaxson a quick nod—Jared would live.

If they got out.

Priority on the prisoners! Jaxson mentally shouted. A few of his pack were still engaged with the guards, but most were cutting the ties of the prisoners. Jaxson clutched his arm to cap the bleeding, then hustled toward the door at the back of the hangar, hoping like crazy there were actually vehicles outside. When he slammed the door open, two white vans shone in the moonlight.

Out the back! he commanded, and the pack moved as one, leaving the guards they were fighting and half carrying the prisoners as they fled. Jaxson held the door as they streamed out of the hangar and to the van. He waited for the last of them to struggle through. The two guards still moving were scrabbling around their fallen compatriots. One came up with a gun, which he pointed at the last of the escaping prisoners.

Jaxson yanked the final one through the door as the shots pinged the sheet metal. He sprinted with him to the vans, catching up with the last prisoners loading in.

"Go! Go! Go!" he shouted as he pulled the van doors shut behind him. The guards probably wouldn't pursue them, but Jaxson didn't want any last-minute casualties, not with vans full of civilians.

They were crammed in—Murphy was driving, Daniel riding shotgun with a couple female civilians jammed in with him, including one on his lap. The back was cramped with seven more prisoners, half of them bleeding. But they made room for Jared, who was laid out on the floor with Jace bending over him. The rough bounce of the van worked against Jaxson as he stumbled to kneel by his brothers.

"Is he all right?" Jaxson asked Jace.

"He will be." Jace's lack of flippant answer made Jaxson's stomach clench. "He needs to be sewn up, which I can't do until we pull over and sit still for a while."

JAXSON

"Murphy!" Jaxson called. "What's our ETA to parking?"

"Need some distance, boss!"

"Copy that," he threw back. "We also need some surgery. ETA!"

There was silence for a moment—Daniel was consulting the GPS. "Four minutes to a good spot to go to ground," he shouted above the tire crunching and creaking of the van. A good, hard bounce forced a groan out of Jared, but then the ride went smooth. They were back on paved road.

Jace was an Army medic and had stitched up more humans and shifters than almost anyone Jaxson knew. "Four minutes?" Jaxson asked. Would it be enough?

Jace gave him a nod. "Four minutes."

Jaxson tipped his head to the bleeding prisoners behind him. "Tend to the others." They had been in Agent Smith's custody—their injuries were probably minor, but God only knew what Smith did to them before Jaxson's pack freed them.

But Jace didn't move, just eyed Jaxson's shoulder, which he was still holding. "You all right?"

"I'm fine." And he was. The bullet took another chunk out of his shoulder in the exact spot where the last one was still healing—so it hurt like hell. And probably aggravated the previous wound. He wasn't quite sure what Smith had injected in him to suppress his wolf, otherwise he wouldn't have even bothered trying to staunch the flow of blood.

Jace nodded and eased up from Jared's side, moving to one of the prisoners to check them over. Jaxson settled on the bare-metal floor of the van next to his injured brother. Jared's breathing had way too much rattle in it. Shifters healed pretty damn fast, but if the magic of their wolves was repressed... Jaxson didn't know how much of that would carry over to Jared's healing powers. They could still communicate mentally as a pack, so Jaxson was counting on there being enough magic left in Jared's blood to keep him from dying—at least until Jace could sew him up. Then, even a small amount of magic would take him the rest of the way.

Jaxson laid a hand on his brother's shoulder, which caused him to drag open his squeezed-shut eyes.

Jared peered up at him. "Still here?"

He didn't know if he meant *Jared* was still here—as in not quite fulfilling his death wish yet—or if *Jaxson* was still by his side. Which he would be until Jared was up and walking again.

"Still here." Jaxson shook his head. "And, by the way, you do *not* have permission to check out, soldier."

Jared nodded, but even in the dim moonlight falling through the front and back windows of the van, Jaxson could see it was shaky.

"Yeah, all right," Jared said. "I guess I'll stick around a while."

"Damn straight." Jaxson choked up a little, which surprised him. Usually, the emotional stuff didn't catch up until well after the fight. "Look, let's get something straight here. All this shit went down because of you. We do all of this *together,* all right? No more lone wolf crap, for fuck's sake. I can't afford to lose you."

Jared huffed a short laugh, then winced and stopped. "You don't need me, bro."

Jaxson dropped his voice and edged closer, dipping his head down to talk quietly with his brother. "I *do* need you, Jared. And not just because you can shoot your way out of a cluster of armed paramilitary guards."

Jared snorted. "Eh, you're just getting soft."

"You're probably right about that." Jaxson grimaced. But he really did need Jared to pull through this. To stick around. Because Jaxson wouldn't be much longer. "And I've got another problem."

"What's that?" Jared looked askance at him.

"I'm in love with Olivia."

Jared's eyebrows lifted, and he didn't say anything for a moment. Jaxson glanced at Jace at the back of the van, talking softly to one of the prisoners. If he heard, he didn't give any sign of it.

"She's not secretly a wolf, is she?" Jared asked, drawing him back. There was surprise in his brother's voice.

Jaxson gave a short laugh. "No." And now wasn't the time to explain she was part witch, either. Being human was bad enough. "She's not a wolf, but she's the best damn thing to happen to me in… well, forever."

Jared listened to him, wide eyed. "You'd leave the pack for her."

"Yes."

Jared nodded, slowly. "Grab her while you can. Don't lose her like I lost Avery. If Olivia's the one, Jaxson, don't fuck it up. Don't let her go."

Jaxson smiled even as his heart ached. "I don't know if I can convince her to have me, but if she will… I'm going spend my life with her."

Jared nodded his approval and shut his eyes. The exertion of even that much talking had visibly depleted him. Jaxson gripped his brother's shoulder and counted the seconds until they could finally stop and sew him up.

He would make sure everyone was healed and recovered and safe.

Then he was going after the woman he loved.

Chapter 18

Olivia was back in her apartment, pacing. Waiting.

Praying that Jaxson would be *able* to call her and tell her everything was fine.

"Seriously, how do you live here?" Her aunt Gwen's disapproval of Olivia's small, very downscale apartment devoid of much in the way of furnishings had manifested as a set of magical drapes, new carpet, and a blue, crushed velvet couch... so far. Olivia didn't know how much of it was glamour, and how much would stay once the glamour wore off.

She prayed the couch wouldn't last.

But she bit her lip for now. She needed Gwen's help to pull this off. Instead, Olivia went for pumping up the pity her aunt obviously felt for her situation. "Foster care taught me to live light. Not get invested in things. You never know when you'll have to pick up and move."

Gwen's look of distress was more than Olivia bargained for.

"It's okay, really," she rushed out. "I like it this way."

"It is *not* okay." Her aunt stopped conjuring knickknacks for the shelves she had just created across Olivia's bare walls in order to stalk over to her. "And this plan of yours is utter foolishness! You can still walk away from..." Gwen gestured around her. "...all of this. There are other men in the world. Let this shifter go and come back with me to the coven. You'd be more than welcome! The sisters would love to have the long-lost daughter of Rowan Damon return. Let me train you. Let me help you conjure a better life. You *deserve* it, dear. You deserve better than all of this."

It was the same argument Gwen had been making all evening, as she fussed with Olivia's apartment and kept her company while they waited for Jaxson's pack to return... *if* they would return. But Olivia believed in him. If there was anyone on the planet who could do this—rescue his brother from the hands of whoever was tormenting their fellow shifters—Jaxson was the man for the job. And that's what made it so worthwhile to take the risk for him.

Gwen may think Olivia deserved a better life, simply because she was her niece, but Jaxson had *earned* a better life with all he'd done—with all he *was*—and Olivia's life would finally *mean something* by giving him the one thing he couldn't get on his own: freedom from the curse.

Olivia took her aunt's hands in hers—something she had a feeling witches rarely did, judging by the wide-eyed look on her aunt's face. "Aunt Gwen, I have to do this. You, better than probably anyone, should understand. My parents *died* because of this thing I have inside me. You have to let me take this chance to make that count for something. To do something with this magic inside me that makes a difference. If it's truly strong enough—if *I'm* strong enough—I'll live through it, just like Sybil said. And if I'm not... then I'll still have freed Jaxson. My life will have mattered. Please don't take that from me."

Her aunt clenched her teeth. Magical fire stormed in her eyes. "Your mother, if she were alive, would turn me to ash for allowing this."

"If my mother were alive, it wouldn't be necessary." Olivia held her gaze, unflinching.

Gwen's shoulders sagged. "All right. I'll do everything I can to help you, Olivia, but... I don't know if I'll be able to save you." The last part was a whisper.

Olivia was asking a lot of her aunt—she knew that. She threw her arms around her neck and hugged her hard. "I know, Aunt Gwen. And just by trying, you're single-handedly proving to me how amazing some witches can be." Olivia released her and leaned back. "If I make it through this, I'm going to join the coven and go all badass witch on you. Just wait and see." And this time, she actually meant that.

Her aunt gave a choked laugh, even though her eyes were glassy with tears.

Olivia's phone buzzed from where it sat on the edge of the now-blue couch.

She froze, staring at it for a second, then lunged over to snatch it up and answer the call. "Hello?"

"Hello, gorgeous." It was Jaxson.

Relief flooded her body. "Jaxson! Are you okay? Is Jared all right? What happened? Tell me! Talk, man, talk!"

He chuckled on the other end. "Man, it's good to hear your voice." He pulled in a breath. "We're fine. All good. Jared took a bullet pretty hard, but Jace sewed him up, and he's fine now."

"Oh, thank God." Olivia let out a breath. "Where are you?"

"Everyone's at the safehouse for now. We gave the bad guys a pretty good smackdown, but the asshole in charge is still on the loose. I need you to come to the safehouse. Everyone connected to this needs to lay low, stay off the radar, until we can get this sorted once and for all."

"The safehouse?" Olivia asked, giving a pointed look to Gwen.

Her aunt's eyes grew wide, and she shook her head rapidly. No way Olivia could bring a witch into a den of wolves. And besides, Olivia couldn't carry out her plan with that many onlookers.

"It's really just my family's place in the mountains. But it's off the grid and safe. And... plenty big. You could have your own room." There was apology in his voice. "I know things aren't exactly settled between us, Olivia, but you have to let me keep you safe. *Please.* Either way, you need to get out of your apartment. Once they get regrouped, they might find you there."

"I..." She scrambled for a reason not to do this. "I have a bunch of work in the office that I'm in the middle of—"

"It can wait." Weariness crept into Jaxson's voice. It was late. He had to be tired from the mission to rescue his brother. And stressed, worrying about her.

Olivia hated using that against him, but she had to. "Look, if we're going to hole up for a long time, I need something to do. And Riverwise needs to keep running while you're hiding out. I'll just stop by the office and pick up a few things—"

"Fine." He was frustrated. "But not without me. I'll meet you there in twenty minutes. Pack up your things and bring everything you'll need for an extended stay. I don't know how long it will take to track these bastards down."

His voice was even more tired now, but she had known he would never let her go to the office alone. Which meant she, Gwen, and Jaxson would be in the same room for a short period of time... and that was all she needed.

"Thank you, Jaxson." The gratitude in her voice was real.

"Olivia." The way he said her name, soft and yearning, choked her up all of a sudden. There was a brief silence on the phone. He seemed to be struggling for words. "I was thinking about you tonight, and—"

"I'll see you there," Olivia said quickly, then hung up the phone. The choking feeling threatened to crawl up and push tears down her face, but she held it in. Whatever Jaxson was going to say, she couldn't hear it... not before she carried through with this. Afterward, he would be free to choose from all the female wolves in the world—she didn't want him professing his love for her *now,* minutes before she freed him from the curse.

JAXSON

It wasn't fair to either of them.

"Are you all right, dear?" The concern was back on Gwen's face.

Olivia swallowed her tears and nodded. "Let's go."

Her glamour had to be *perfect*... only trouble was she hadn't performed any magic in over a decade.

"How do I look?" Olivia asked her aunt. They didn't have any mirrors in her office, which was where they were waiting for Jaxson to arrive.

"Sybil had more cleavage showing." Gwen's nose was wrinkled with disgust.

Olivia could hardly stand it herself, but her glamour spell was supposed to convince Jaxson that his nemesis had returned. She had to get it right. She closed her eyes and pictured the haughty witch in her mind—yes, she definitely had more cleavage showing under her clingy purple silk blouse than Olivia had allowed. Adjusting the glamour was like adjusting her imagination, so as soon as she had a good fix on Sybil's porcelain skin, long raven hair, and oversized breasts straining against the skimpy outfit, Olivia opened her eyes again.

"How's that?" she asked.

"Perfect." Gwen's frown showed her disgust, but at least Olivia had the spell right.

"How do I sound?"

"Your voice is a dead match, but you don't *sound* like her at all," her aunt said.

"Because I'm not rude enough?" Olivia winced. She was a kitten to Sybil's tigress. How was she going to be able to pull this off?

"Imagine you loathe everyone except for the pleasure or power they can bring you." Gwen's expression was even more disgusted. "Talk to me like you're thinking about turning me to ash just for daring to breathe your air. Like you're the Queen of all magic, only no one has managed to appreciate your brilliance."

"Pathetic peasants!" Olivia swept out a hand to her imaginary audience. It was jarring to see it look *exactly* like Sybil's long-fingered one. "Can't you see how glorious I am? You will suffer under my reign!"

Gwen gave her a skeptical look. "A little less… *medieval.*"

"What do I care what *you* think? You're a washed up witch in a dreary little coven."

Gwen looked stricken. "Better."

"Oh my gosh," Olivia rushed out. "I didn't mean that, Aunt Gwen."

She rolled her eyes. "Olivia, dear… you need to *commit* to this ruse to have any chance of making it work. But it's not too late to back out. In fact, I've half a mind to

JAXSON

simply drag you back to my coven and lock you up until this… *insanity* of yours passes."

Olivia pulled herself up to Sybil's full, haughty height. "Try it, *Gwen dear*. We'll see who's the better witch."

Gwen's eyebrows lifted. "Impressive."

The click of the front door was all the warning they had that Jaxson was coming. Gwen waved Olivia back toward her desk so Jaxson wouldn't see her until he was already in the room.

"I'll be right here," she whispered. "If you change your mind at any time—"

"Gwen." Olivia put all of Sybil's disdain into that single word.

Her aunt cringed under it and retreated to the door.

Olivia schooled her expression into one of sultry power—as if she really was Jaxson's old lover, ready to get one last taste of her favorite wolf before setting him free. Her story was simple: Sybil had obtained a better offer for Jaxson's mating bond, and she was looking to parlay that into one last fling with her favorite shifter—something Sybil totally would have done if she was anywhere near as smart as she thought she was.

Jaxson was practically running when he reached the door of her office and hurried right in. "Olivia—"

He stopped cold when his eyes met hers—or rather, *Sybil's*. He growled and swung a quick look around the room. When he saw Gwen at the door, closing it behind him, his growl ramped up to a hair-raising snarl, and his fangs and claws sprang out. Olivia's heart lurched at seeing him this way, and she struggled not to let her sudden fear show.

Jaxson half-crouched and flicked looks between Olivia and Gwen, keeping his distance from them both. "What are you doing here, *witch?*" He spit out the last word.

Olivia steeled her expression. She *was* a full-fledged witch—at least as far as Jaxson knew—and he wouldn't attack her for fear of being turned into ash. His look of loathing and anger, however, was breaking her heart... even though it was really directed at Sybil.

"Why, I've *missed* you, Jaxson," she said, amazed that her voice was at all steady. "And I've got a little proposition for you."

His eyes pinched in suspicion. "What are you talking about, Sybil?" Then his eyes went wide, and he scanned the room again. Now there was plain fear on his face. "What have you done with Olivia?"

"She's safe." It wasn't hard to sound unconcerned. "Sleeping spell. Not far away."

The fear was shoved off his face by a flush of anger three times as strong. He rushed at her, stopping inches away, chest heaving. "If you've hurt her, Sybil, I swear to God, I'll make you pay."

Olivia didn't move a muscle... but only because she was paralyzed by fear. She desperately tried to turn that into the outrage she knew Sybil would have reacted with. "Don't threaten me, little wolf!" She raised a hand, and he flinched away, backing up two steps.

The anger still seethed on his face, but he was holding himself back. No doubt because he thought Sybil could kill him with a single touch.

Olivia lowered her hand. "That's better. You'll have your little human toy back soon enough." She swallowed. "Assuming we can make a deal."

"What kind of deal?" His claws and fangs slowly retracted. He glanced at Gwen and frowned, clearly wondering who she was and why she was here. He turned back to Olivia. "You've already ruined my life with your curse, Sybil. What more do you want?"

"Ah, yes, the curse. That's why I'm here, my sexy little Jaxson." Olivia cocked her head to the side, trying for sultry but afraid she just looked demented. She breathed a sigh of relief inside—they were finally getting to the point.

"What the fuck are you talking about?" His glare was murderous, even though he was holding back. "Out with it, Sybil. Then tell me what you've done with Olivia."

"*So* impatient," Olivia said, drawing it out the way she imagined Sybil would. "It's quite simple, my delicious one. It seems another witch has taken a fancy to you, and she would like you released from your curse."

"Another witch?" His brow furrowed.

"Yes, she works with one of your clients." Olivia waved a hand in the air and pulled a name from Riverwise's accounting. "Mr. Talos or something. What matters is she thinks you're just her type, but she divined my mark upon you. She's a fool, clearly, and was willing to pay far more than you're worth, but we've worked out an arrangement."

The confusion on Jaxson's face deepened. "You're saying you've sold me to another witch?" He glanced at Gwen, new fear on his face.

"No, no… not *Guinevere*. She's my assistant." Olivia waved at her aunt as if dismissing her, then she slowly stepped toward Jaxson, swaying her hips as much as she could without being completely awkward. "But once I release you from the curse, you should high-tail it out of Seattle, little wolf. Before Ismarelda can find you."

Jaxson had been backing up in equal measure, but he stopped. "Release me?"

Olivia sauntered closer. "All you have to do is sink those sexy fangs of yours into me, and poof…" She fluttered her fingers. "Goodbye, curse."

"You want me to *bite* you?" His bewildered look threatened to throw the whole ruse.

"Well, yes. I'm here because the bite is necessary. Unbreakable magic bonds, blah, blah, blah... I don't expect your little wolfy mind to comprehend it all. Trust me that a bite is all I require to break the curse." She looked him up and down as lasciviously as she could. "But a little gratitude for my sacrifice would be a delicious way for you to say thank you."

He narrowed his eyes at her and threw another glance at Gwen, who was remaining as still as a statue, blank-faced, giving nothing away. "I didn't think you were into threesomes, Sybil."

Olivia sighed dramatically. *"Fine.* You're really no fun now that you're all grown up, Jaxson. I'll settle for just the bite. Let's get this over with." She tilted her head to the side, baring her neck to him. Her heart thudded in her chest, but she held as absolutely still as she could manage.

Jaxson edged toward her until he was less than a foot away, but he was still acting as if she were a live electrical wire. "Why are you doing this, Sybil?" he asked quietly, expression still confused.

She gave him an impatient look. "There are things I want more than *you,* little wolf. Your curse has become *inconvenient."*

He nodded, still frowning, but closed the distance between them. His fangs grew until they were long and sharp and poised over her shoulder. He hesitated again. "Once I do this, you'll tell me where you're keeping Olivia."

"Yes." It was getting difficult to hide her heaving breaths. Fear was racing through her. This was it. This was her chance. Her first, last, and only chance. But only if Jaxson took the bait.

He grabbed her hair, roughly, bending her head even farther to the side… and sunk his fangs into her. The twin points pierced her skin and sent electric shocks racing through her body. She gasped and grabbed tightly onto him—the glamour had already vaporized, and it was only a matter of seconds before he would realize who she was. She had to make sure the bite took… but she only held him for a moment before her hold started to slip. Inky blackness flooded from her shoulder, weighing her down with impossible heaviness, rushing her head and making it hard to hold up. The darkness rushed her eyes and stole her sight. She felt her body go slack and heard the thump of it hitting the ground more than felt it… because everything was numb, so numb, and she was spiraling down and down and…

I'm a witch.

The thought fought against the thick sludge of the curse seeping through every cell of her body. *I'm a witch and I have power and I can fight this.*

JAXSON

That thought dredged up something, some blue light from deep inside her. It did battle against the sludge the way a sunbeam fights through the fog. She urged it on, pushed it, tried for more, and for a brief shining moment, some of the darkness cleared.

She fought to open her eyes, still sealed shut with the heaviness of her body. Through heavy lids, she could see Jaxson hovering above her, shouting soundless words, horror on his face.

"Jaxson." Her lips moved, but no air was passing through them, so no sound left them. *Jaxson, I love you.* She wished that thought could reach him somehow. But the darkness had crawled back up from the depths, shimmying the edges of her soul to grab her and drag her back down with it.

Back into the dark.

She wasn't strong enough after all.

CHAPTER 19

"*Olivia!*" Jaxson couldn't believe his eyes.

One moment he was sinking his fangs into Sybil, the next he had Olivia collapsing in his arms and falling to the floor. She was convulsing and twitching in the most horrifying way, and just as he realized, *holy fuck, I bit Olivia,* the other witch came along and literally shoved him away. He was so stunned, it took him a moment to react.

Then he was back with a fury. "What have you done to her!"

The witch shot a hand at him that he barely dodged.

JAXSON

Blue energy swirled in her palm. *"Do not* interfere, wolf!"

"What the fuck is going on?" Jaxson gaped at Olivia. She moaned and struggled to open her eyes... and failed. "What is *happening* to her?" Tears pressed against the back of his eyes.

"She's dying from your bite, you fool!" She spit out the words, but all her focus was on the blue energy dripping from her hand and melting all around Olivia's head. But it didn't touch her, just pooled on the floor around her body.

Jaxson's heart and mind were spinning, but the pieces quickly fell into place: *Olivia had tricked him.* She was half witch. For some reason, she had used a spell to pretend she was Sybil to get him to bite her. And now she was dying from the poison in his bite.

But why? "Why would she do this?" he whispered out loud, as much to himself as to the witch.

But she still answered, muttering as her hands floated over Olivia. "Because she was stupid enough to fall in love with a wolf. A *cursed* wolf. Only my sister's daughter could be this stubborn *and* foolish at the same time." Then the witch cursed in some ancient language—or maybe it was a spell. The energy pulsing from her hand turned green and continued to swirl around Olivia.

"Can you save her?" He didn't really understand what was happening, but the only thing that mattered was keeping Olivia from dying.

"I'm trying, wolf, now shut up." The witch muttered some more words in that strange language, then said, "Dammit!" She clapped her hands together, dissipating the green magic, then rocked back on her heels. Olivia's body was still twitching, but less so. Not because she was getting better... because her face was slowly turning gray. The witch's shoulders sagged.

Jaxson looked between Olivia and the witch. "You have to keep trying!"

"There's nothing more I can do." There were tears in her eyes—she meant it.

No, no, please, no. He reached shaky hands to Olivia's cheeks, but she wasn't moving anymore, and her beautiful skin was clammy to the touch. All this time, he'd done everything he could to keep the curse from finding its target. To keep some innocent woman from paying the price for his foolishness. And now, just as he'd found the one girl who stole his heart with her very first words, even as he tried to shield her from all the dangers in his life, the curse had *still* found her.

"Nooo!" he roared. All the fury and pain of his inner wolf came to the surface, and he nearly let his beast loose. The pain of this was *too much*. But he couldn't give up. *Refused* to give up. He turned to the witch. "There has to be something you can do!"

JAXSON

"Do you think I would hold back?" she hissed at him. "She's my niece! If I could save her, I would. This is *your* fault wolf! And hers for wanting to free you from your curse!"

That struck him like a cattle prod to the chest. Olivia had been trying to save him... *again.*

"What can I do?" he begged the witch in a whisper filled with pain. "I'll do anything. Just tell me what to do. I can't let her... she can't do this!"

The witch narrowed her eyes. "Anything?"

"Yes!" Olivia's utter stillness drew his attention. For all he could tell, she was already dead. He thrust both wrists toward the witch. "Take my life! Give it to her. You're a *witch*. You can do any goddamn thing." He was fighting to keep back the tears because he knew that wasn't really true. They had limits. Witches were insanely strong in magic, but they couldn't conquer death. They couldn't bring someone back if it was too late.

The witch was nodding and looking quickly between him and Olivia. "It might be possible," she whispered. Then she grabbed hold of one of his wrists and took Olivia's in the other. The witch fixed him with an intense look. "I can transfer some of your magic to her. The healing properties may be enough to save her."

"Do it!" His eyes were wide. Was this really possible?

She mumbled a few words, briefly closed her eyes, and

kept her grip on his wrist rock-hard. At first, he didn't feel anything. Then it hit him like a white-hot poker had stabbed him in the back. He arched, holding in the scream that wanted to work loose, but he couldn't help the groan that escaped. The pain went on and on, like a cleaving of his soul in two, half remaining howling inside his body, the other gushing in a stream through his wrist and the witch's touch. After the shock of it passed, he welcomed the screaming pain, the gut-wrenching torment. It was only right that *he* be the one to pay for this. He would give all he had—*all in, all the time*—to save her. He prayed through the agony: *please God, let this work.*

Suddenly the pain was gone, disappearing like a switch cutting off. Jaxson slumped on the floor, dizzy, but... he was still alive. He whipped his head back to Olivia. Her aunt was bent over her, and she was moving again, shaking her head, eyes still squeezed shut.

But she was alive.

Jaxson's whole body sagged with relief.

Olivia's aunt twisted to give Jaxson a hard look. "Do you love her?" It was a tight whisper, and Olivia was still fighting to wake up.

Jaxson straightened quickly. "Yes," he said without hesitation.

"Good. The magic will take better that way."

He frowned because he didn't understand any of the

JAXSON

details on this. And Olivia still wasn't awake. "Is she all right?"

The witch released Olivia's cheeks, conjured another ball of blue magic, and dripped it over her. "Yes, but she still has to fight her way back from the brink. I can help her with that. Boost her own magic, mixed with yours, to kill off the last of the poison magic." The witch peered at him as her hands floated over Olivia. "She was near death, Jaxson. Your magic saved her."

He let out a breath. "You're sure?"

"I'm sure," she said, her face serious. "But you need to know something before she wakes—she'll forever have a connection to you now."

"Because she carries my magic." He looked at Olivia's face with wonder. The gray of death was rapidly fading, replace by her normal rosy skin color.

"Yes. It's not quite a mating bond, but..." She looked expectantly at him.

"But she's a witch. They don't bond... do they?" The wolf inside him had perked all the way up. This was... this was impossible and amazing and... *perfect*. If it were real.

"Not normally," the witch said. "But Olivia was half witch, half human."

Jaxson nodded. "Her human side can bond."

"If you choose it." Her eyes narrowed. "You're still

free to choose another mate. A shifter mate. And I hear your kind can mate more with more than one female."

Jaxson snarled his disgust. "*My* kind mates for life. With one woman."

Olivia was rousing, squinting her eyes, and sucking in a breath.

The witch nodded and whispered quickly, "No matter what, she's forever connected to you. But if you don't want her for a mate, tell me *now*, wolf. And *leave us*. I will tell her you're free of the curse, off to seek your true mate, and then I'll bring her back to my coven. Her sisters will give her a new home. We'll care for her, give her everything she needs. We'll teach her to be the witch she was always meant to be."

Jaxson stared at her, mouth hanging open during her furtive offer. "I'm not going *anywhere*. If she'll have me, I'm hers. *Already*. And now..." He gazed at her beautiful face as she opened her eyes. "Now she's given me something I had never dared to dream was possible."

The witch seemed to scan the air around his head—reading his aura, like Sybil used to. All she would find there was that he was telling the truth.

She smiled a little. "I was hoping that might be your answer." The witch turned to help Olivia up to sitting, but Jaxson was instantly on the other side, lifting her up and pulling her into his lap.

"Jaxson." Olivia's voice was shaky and breathy. She peered up into his eyes. "Did it work?"

He brushed her disheveled hair back from her face. "Getting rid of the curse? Yes. Your attempt to die for me? No." He couldn't hold back his smile anymore, and it stretched his face with all the joy bursting out of him.

A shudder ran through her, the leftovers of the trauma. "Oh, thank God." Her shaky hand found his shirt and bunched it in her fist. Then she leaned her head against his chest, still breathing hard. He closed his arms around her, holding her tight and safe. The feel of her in his arms was like nothing he'd ever felt in his life. Happiness. Gratitude. An unfathomable connection, even without the skin-to-skin contact that had been so magical before.

That probably *was* magic, now that he thought about it.

The woman who was Olivia's aunt rose up from the floor. She gave Jaxson a tiny smile and an even more subtle tip of the head before she slipped out the door.

He would find a way to thank her... later.

For now, he was absorbed by the woman in his arms.

His true mate.

She was *alive*.

Olivia could hardly believe it. *It worked!* As the final shakes of the battle against the poison left her body, she reveled in this closeness with Jaxson. It might be the last time she could have his arms so securely around her. He was grateful to her for releasing him from the curse, and she would take any hugs he might want to give for that. Happiness flooded her body like a drug, making her heart soar. *She had done good...* and she had used magic to do it. It was freeing, lifting the burden she'd carried all these years—and it was enough to permanently anchor that happiness in her heart. It would even be enough to float her through the coming time when Jaxson would move on. Now that he was free, it would take no time for him to find the perfect mate. And she would be happy for him. Heartbroken, but strangely... *truly happy.*

Because he would finally have all he would need to keep that smile forever on his face.

She untucked her head from his chest and peered up into his face. *He looked so happy!* It made her smile. She gently touched his cheek. There were healing scars and bruises on it, the badges of honor and courage he carried from saving his brother, no doubt. Because that was the kind of man Jaxson River was.

"I can hardly believe it worked," she breathed. "Good thing Gwen was able to bring me back, though. I don't think I would have made it without her."

JAXSON

"Gwen didn't bring you back." He smirked, the joy still on his face. "I did."

She frowned her confusion. "What do you mean?"

"Your aunt transferred some of my magic—the magic in my blood—to you." His eyes shone as he said this.

Olivia straightened up and leaned away to get a better look at him. "You *what?* How is that... is that even possible?"

He shrugged. "She used some spell—I don't know what it was—but believe me, I felt every second of it." He bit his lip and raked his eyes over her body. "And now, there's part of me that will forever be inside you."

She frowned and worked her way out of his lap, scooting a couple feet away. She wanted to stand, get some distance from him, figure this thing out... but her legs were too shaky to trust. "What does that even mean?" Dread trickled through her heart. Had he foiled her attempt to free him with a last-ditch attempt to save her?

The joy fell off his face, but his eyes stayed glued to hers. "It means you're forever bound, magically, to me. A part of *me* is inside of *you.*"

The dread found its way to her face. "Like a *mating?*"

Pain winced across his face. "It doesn't have to be. It could be like the connection I have with my brothers. Or my pack. But we *are* connected... I guess you *could* be like a sister to me, if that's what you want. But Olivia…" The pain doubled on his face. "I want so much more than sisterly love from you."

Oh no. "No, no, no." She backed away from him, shaking her finger at him. "You need to find a *real* mate. One who's a shifter! One who can give you pups and bind your pack together and let you lead Riverwise!" Tears were working her way to her face, despite her effort to keep them buried. "That was the *whole point*, Jaxson! To free you to find your *true* mate!"

He blinked and dropped his gaze to the floor, not meeting her accusing look. "This is about the boyfriend, isn't it?"

"No!" she cried. "This is about *you*… and giving you what you need to be happy!"

His head whipped up. *"You* are what makes me happy." He crossed the floor between them, crawling on his hands and knees to reach her but stopping just short of touching her. His face was inches from hers. *"You*, Olivia Lilyfield, are everything I've always wanted in a mate. Everything I thought I would never have."

"But you have to save your pack—"

"My pack will survive. Riverwise will go on. It's *you* that I can't live without." Tears were glassing his eyes, and it nearly broke Olivia's heart on the spot. "Tell me you love this boyfriend of yours. That you love him *more* than me. Because I *know* there's some part of you that loves me. But if you tell me it's not enough... if you tell me to leave... I'll go."

She was shaking again, but with a torment she could barely describe. Something inside her—something strong and magical and born of love—was crying out for her to take him in her arms. It took everything she had to hold herself back, but... the words slipped out without her permission.

"There is no boyfriend." She sucked in a breath.

His eyes flashed, and suddenly she was flat on her back on the floor with Jaxson looming over her. He had that hungry look again, like he wanted to take her, consume her, claim her. It fired a visceral response through every part of her body, igniting her everywhere at once.

His chest was heaving. "Say you love me."

"I love you." She was equally breathless.

He lowered himself down to her, still not touching, but panting even harder. "Say you want me."

"I want you." She couldn't help herself. It was true, and with him looking at her like that—

"Olivia Lilyfield, I want you for my mate. To hold and love and protect. *Forever.* Please, God, say yes."

She swallowed. She could barely breathe. But she couldn't say *no* to him, not like this. Not ever again.

"Yes," she breathed.

His lips and body crashed down on hers, claiming her with his urgent need to kiss her, touch her, have her for his own. Her heart soared again, and the magic inside her rejoiced at his nearness and his touch. That spark she had always felt racing across her skin whenever he touched her now thrilled through her entire body. Every molecule of her *belonged* to him. *With him.*

He pulled back, breathless from their kiss, to gaze into her eyes. "Olivia, I want you so badly," he whispered.

Her hands found his face, touched his cheeks, dug into his hair. "How does this even work?" she breathed. "I don't understand what we're doing."

He flashed a smile. "That's because we're doing something entirely new." He was still breathing hard. "But you're truly my mate, in every real sense of the word. Our pups will be… *different*… but strong. I can feel it. Can you?"

"*Yes.*" She nodded to back it up. Because she *could*. There was something inside her that *knew*—anything that came from their love would have *his* strength and *hers*. And she had a powerful magic inside her. One she no longer feared. It was given to her by her mother, and she would pass it on to their children. She would teach them how to use it—safely. And she would love them with the same bright, shining love she had for their father.

"*Jaxson.*" It was almost too much for her heart to contain. "Is it possible to die from happiness? Because I think I might."

He grinned. "No one is dying tonight. But I'm going to claim you, Olivia Lilyfield, right here, right now. And I fully expect that to take both of us to heaven and back."

She gasped as he dove back into kissing her, claiming first her mouth, then planting urgent kisses on her neck. His growl rumbled in his chest, but it was pressed so close to hers, that it vibrated her entire body. The heat between her legs was going to melt her entire body, and everywhere he touched as he literally ripped through her clothes, slicing and tearing them from her body, was a flashpoint of desire and longing. She was naked in seconds. His hands were hot on her body, leaving only to shove his own clothes out of the way of their ability to touch *everywhere.* The magic surging inside her yearned for every second of it, and before she could even voice her need for him, he was plunging his cock inside her. It was rough and fast, and he was large and hard, it immediately tripped her higher than she'd ever been.

"Oh God, Olivia," he panted as he thrust inside her again and again, taking her hard against the floor, sliding her body a little each time with the force of it.

She clung to him, riding his passion, digging her hands into his back and calling his name incoherently. He filled her completely, stretching her wide and grinding a pleasure out of her that pushed her quickly to the brink.

"Jaxson!" she shrieked as she came, her body arching against his, fighting his urgent thrusts while dying to have him even closer and deeper inside her. Wave after wave consumed her, and it was like no orgasm she had ever experienced. She didn't even know if it was an orgasm—more like happiness and love exploding inside her. It was heaven, just as he said—a magical one that was unearthly and threatened to float her right out of her body on waves of pleasure.

He stopped suddenly, pulling out and looming above her. His eyes were wild, animal-like, and hooded with lust. "Turn over," he commanded.

It didn't occur to her to even question it.

Jaxson's wolf was growling with need so loud, he could barely hear anything else.

Olivia's gorgeous body was writhing underneath him, and he reveled in her pleasure, her body squeezing tightly down on his cock on wave after wave of her pleasure, but he needed *more* from her. He and his wolf both needed to *claim her*.

She already owned his heart and mind. And his magic was already swimming in her veins. She *already* belonged to him. But the man and wolf in him both needed to sink his fangs into her while taking her in the lust-filled frenzy of a true claiming—a *mating*—the way he'd always heard of, always dreamed about in his hottest, wildest fantasies, but never thought would be a reality for him. And now, because of this brave, incredible woman before him, he was going to have his ultimate dream become his real life.

"Turn over." He could barely growl out the words through his *need* for her clouding his mind.

She didn't hesitate, just like before, turning over and offering herself to him. He grabbed hold of her gorgeous, curvy hips, allowing his claws to come out, just a little, just enough to mark her in the tiniest of ways—a small pain that should only drive her pleasure higher. Her gasp made his already rock-hard cock twitch, and he was aching to plunge inside her again. His fangs grew, and the magic pooled in his mouth. He gripped her hips and thrust hard inside her. She let out a shriek that every fiber of his being responded to. He pounded into her again and again, building her pleasure and his. She writhed and squirmed against his hold, driving him to impossible heights. He wasn't going to be able to hold out much longer.

He bent over her, thrusting deeper and harder as he hovered closer to her, positioning himself so he could claim her simultaneously with his cock and his bite. *And his love.* She whimpered under him, and he could feel her muscles clenching around his cock. *So close.*

"You are *mine*," he whispered, his voice hoarse with need.

"Yes," she panted.

"Forever mine." His words were stronger now, the magic surging in him.

"Yes, please, God, take me, Jaxson." Her words were tumbling over one another.

It was more than he could take.

He buried his cock deep inside, released her hip, grabbed her hair and pulled her head to the side, baring her sweet, beautiful neck to his fangs. He pierced her skin, just enough to cause that last push of pain… and to release the magic into her blood. She wasn't a shifter—he couldn't ravish her with his bite without concern for recovery—so he was careful not to go too deep with his fangs. His cock made up for that by shoving as far and as deep into her as he could go.

She shrieked with pleasure and came around him, squeezing down on him and pushing him over the edge. Wave after wave pulsed through him as he emptied himself into her—his seed, his magic, his love. His wolf howled in triumph. The magic surged and strengthened inside him. He was alpha even *more*. To his infinite surprise, it *was* a true claiming, her love and her magic strengthening his wolf in a way that seemed impossible... but was undeniably true.

He kept thrusting, kept riding her, kept wringing out the last waves of her pleasure and his until they were both completely and totally spent. Then he withdrew his fangs and his cock, all at once, collapsing on the carpet next to her and drawing her down to the floor with him.

"Oh my God, Jaxson," she breathed.

His smile almost broke him, it was so strong. "Did you enjoy that, my love?"

"Holy... what *was* that?" She was still panting.

He pulled her closer, snuggling her back against him so he could fondle her amazingly gorgeous breasts—there had been nowhere near enough of *that* before now. He made a note to start there next time.

"That," he growled into her hair, "was one hell of a claiming, my love. *Goddammit,* you are one sexy, hot witch."

She peered at him, over her shoulder, with wide eyes. "Tell me it's going to be like that every time." She gasped between the words.

"No, my love." He grinned. "It's only going to get better with time."

She closed her eyes and mouthed a silent *thank you*, and he couldn't help the rumble of laughter that shook its way out of him. Then his gaze fell on the twin fang marks at the crook of her neck. He thought he might have to get her some bandages or some kind of first aid, just to make sure she was all right, but before his wondering eyes, the wound magically healed.

He gaped a little, but then he realized, *of course*. His magic had already healed her, already brought her back from death. A simple puncture wound should be nothing.

He slid her around to face him and cupped her cheeks in his hands, causing her to open her eyes again. "How in the name of magic did I get so lucky as to have you in my life?" he asked. And he meant it in all sincerity. She had saved him in every way and given him more than he ever thought possible.

But she didn't answer him, she just shook her head. "I've never felt this… *complete* before. I didn't think…" Her eyes were tearing up. "I didn't think a family was something I would ever have. And I know your family may not want a witch in it, but if all I ever have is you in my arms, that's all I'll ever need."

He frowned. Because she could be right—his family might not accept her—but that was the last thing he wanted her thinking right now. "You don't worry about that," he said. "I'll take care of everything. In fact…" He kissed her, hard, trying to banish that thought from her mind. "I only have one question for you: what's your previous record for the number of orgasms you've experienced in a twenty-four hour period?"

She laughed, and it filled his heart. "Is that something I should be tracking?"

"Oh yes." He slid his hand over the luscious mound of her breast and down between her legs. Her breath caught in a way that coursed satisfaction through him. "Whatever it is, we're going to double it." His fingers plunged inside the slick wetness of her sex, causing her head to tip back against him, and her eyes to drift closed. He could take her higher than she'd ever gone, again and again, an infinite number of times over a lifetime together, and it would never be enough to repay her for all she had given him.

But he sure as hell was going to try.

CHAPTER 20

"It's time, Olivia." Jaxson's voice was gentle, but it still ramped up her anxiety.

"Are you sure? Maybe we should wait." The last twenty-four hours were a whirlwind—filled with more orgasms than she could count, but that was all before they arrived at the "safehouse," otherwise known as a sprawling stone and redwood estate in the Washington mountains owned by Jaxson's family. Since they'd arrived, she'd had her own room. She'd slept for about ten hours after they'd landed in the middle of the night before, so it wasn't like she'd even been conscious in the safehouse for more than a couple hours. Long enough to get some food and say hello to the assortment of shifters populating the estate, now that they were all hiding out from this "Agent Smith" Jaxson had told her about. He and his brothers would find that guy and put him out of the business of kidnapping and experimenting on shifters soon, but for now, they were laying low and making plans.

And, apparently, telling Jaxson's family that they had mated.

Jaxson drew her into his arms, running his hands through her hair and kissing her gently on the forehead. "I can't wait any longer," he said. "I need everyone to know that you're mine, so when I drag you back to my room, and your screams of pleasure rock the walls, they'll understand."

"Jaxson!" She pulled back and gave him an incredulous look. "You are *not* doing that. I would die of embarrassment."

"I am *so* doing that." He smirked at her discomfort like it didn't bother him in the least. "Precisely *no one* will be surprised. But if it really concerns you, we'll use the bridal suite my mom keeps out in back, near the stables."

She scowled at him, but she couldn't keep it going for long. He was just so damn adorable and oozing with hotness. How could she complain about him wanting to drag her off and make wild love to her?

"Your mom has already been really nice to me." Mrs. River had fixed a special meal for Olivia as soon as she had dragged herself out of her room. "But that's all going to change when she finds out what I am."

Jaxson's grin faded. "There's no love of witches in this house. I know that. And to some extent, that's earned. But you're no ordinary witch." His fingers traced her jawline, then tucked a stray piece of hair behind her ear. The love in his eyes made her heart melt… and the magic in her body surge. "You're my *mate*," he whispered. "They'll have to accept you or lose me. Either way, you and I are *together*. A team. They'll recognize that as soon as they see us. It's up to them to decide what to do with it."

She nodded, but her heart still clenched at the idea of Jaxson losing *anything* over her.

He gently kissed her again, this time on the lips. Her heart swelled with the tenderness of it. "No matter what," he said, "when this is all over, I'm taking you away for a while. Somewhere quiet where we can just be ourselves and not worry about the world. How does that sound?"

She pulled back to look into his eyes. "Like heaven."

He grinned and took her hand, tipping his head toward the main room down the hall. "Let's get this over with."

Olivia pulled in a deep breath of courage and held his hand tight as they strode down the hallway. The River estate was decorated in a wonderfully rustic style—rough-hewn log and white stone walls, woven throw rugs over polished wooden floors, and the scent of the mountains drifting into every room. The walls held portraits of the scenic mountains and wildlife, but you only had to look out the windows to see it for real. She imagined it was *perfect* for an extended family of shifters to call home.

She just didn't know how she would ever fit in.

When they rounded the corner to the great room, she sucked in a sharp breath. Jaxson's entire pack must be here—between the floor-to-ceiling window at one end and the two-story stone fireplace at the other, there were more than two dozen shifters. She recognized Murphy and Rich and Taylor, as well as the others from Riverwise. Jared and Jace stood nearby, with their mother between them. Even a few of the Wildings hung out at the edges of the room, where it opened up to a vast dining room capable of seating dozens.

Olivia swallowed and held tighter to Jaxson's hand.

"Thanks, everyone, for coming," Jaxson started.

Even though he was the one talking, Olivia felt like all eyes were glued to her. She kept her gaze on Jaxson's face, strong and confident, standing before all his friends and family and pack about to tell them his darkest secret. It made her stand a little taller. If *he* could be that brave, the least she could do was stand strong by his side.

"As you know, someone in the government is stalking shifters," Jaxson continued. "I don't know why, but they're performing experiments that mess with our ability to shift, and there's no way that's a good thing for any shifter, whether you're on their radar or not. I'm confident we can ferret out whoever is behind this—we'll expose them to the light of day and bring an end to this crime against shifter-kind. But you're going to need full faith in your alpha in order for us all to work together and defeat this common enemy." He took a breath as he slowly scanned the attentive faces. "To do that, you need to know a secret I've been hiding from all of you for years."

Several furtive glances were exchanged and a murmur rose up.

Jaxson waited a moment before he continued. "When I was sixteen, I made the mistake of letting a witch seduce me." Some eyebrows rose, but the room quieted. "When she couldn't get what she wanted from me, she cursed me. Any mate I claimed… would die." An audible gasp went around the room.

Even from across the room, Olivia could see Terra Wilding's eyes go wide and her face pale.

JAXSON

Jaxson held up a hand to quiet them again. "I should have taken a mate years ago, but because of the curse, I've been stalling. I knew that, eventually, I would have to step down." An angry murmur swelled up this time, with sounds of disagreement and growls mixed in. "I had hoped..." he said loud enough to rise about the noise. "I had hoped that I would be able to carry you through this crisis. But instead, an answer to my problem stumbled into my life." He looked at Olivia then, with an expression so soft, it melted her heart. "An answer I wasn't expecting and would never have dreamed possible." He turned back to them. "Olivia broke the curse."

Another gasp went around, along with frowns of confusion.

"How did she do it?" a voice from the crowd threw out. Olivia searched for the source—it was Jace, standing next to Jaxson's mother, a scowl etched deep in his forehead. "You're talking about a magical curse. How does a human break a curse like that?"

Olivia swallowed. *Here it comes,* she thought. *They're going to toss me out the moment they know the truth.*

"Olivia is half witch." Jaxson's voice was soft, but it carried over the crowd like a gong sounding.

Jace's scowl grew deeper. He crossed his arms and stared hard at Olivia, like he might see the witchy part if he looked hard enough. Olivia tried not to shrink away. He wasn't exactly glaring at her... more like he was trying to figure this whole thing out.

"Olivia used her magic to break the curse," Jaxson continued. "She nearly died last night taking the poison of the curse into her own body and battling it there." He dropped her hand and slipped his arm around her shoulder, drawing her close. "I knew she was brave *before* she did such a stupid thing trying to save me from my own foolishness." He looked back at the gathered shifters. Their faces were mostly blank with shock. "But this thing she did for me... if I hadn't already fallen in love with her, that would have pretty much sealed the deal." He took another breath and blew it out. "And so, we're here to tell you that, last night, I made Olivia my mate."

Jace uncrossed his arms and lurched forward. Jared's hand landed on his shoulder, trying to hold him back, but Jace shook him off.

"How is that even possible?" Jace asked in an angry voice. "You say she's a *witch*. You can't mate with one of those." He glared at her and turned back to Jaxson. "Maybe she didn't save you, Jaxson. Maybe she's put a love curse on you! Maybe this is just her messing with all of us. You *know* how they are."

Jaxson locked gazes with his brother. "I know because

she's carrying my magic in her blood, Jace. I can *feel* her love for me."

His eyebrows flew up. *"What?"*

But instead of replying, Jaxson swept his gaze back to the others. "I'm stepping down as your alpha." He raised a hand toward them. "I release you from your pledges." He dropped his hand. "I always knew this day would come. I fully understand why you wouldn't want an alpha who has mated with a witch, but trust me when I tell you, she hasn't cursed me. She hasn't thrown a love spell over me." He turned to her with love in his eyes. "She's the best damn thing that's ever happened to me, and I'm not letting her go."

The shifters looked uncomfortably at one another, but they were keeping quiet.

Jace lurched forward again, reaching Jaxson and gripping his shoulder hard. *"Think* about what you're doing here," he said quietly, but his face was aghast.

"I know exactly what I'm doing, Jace." Jaxson's voice was calm.

"How can you be sure she hasn't—" Jace was cut off by Jared looming behind him.

"A man knows when he's been cursed." Jared's gruff voice carried over the suddenly quiet crowd. "And he knows when he's found his mate." He edged around Jace to face Olivia. Jared was a mountain of a man, even larger than Jaxson, and Olivia was proud she didn't cower under his intense gaze.

He smiled a little for her, but his booming words were for Jace and the rest of the crowd. "Any woman who saves a brother of mine, much less wins his heart, is a sister to me." Then he reached his muscular arms around her and swept her into a hug.

Olivia had stayed quiet through all of Jaxson's speech, but a squeak escaped her as she was squeezed between Jared's massive, rock-hard chest and his bands-of-iron arms. He released her quickly, but the bashful smile on his face warmed her heart and pushed tears up to her eyes.

She didn't know what to say, but she was spared having to figure it out by the shifters in the crowd. One by one, they were *changing...* they were shifting to their wolf forms and bowing their heads to the floor, tails tucked behind.

Jaxson stood, watching them, his mouth open.

"What's happening?" Olivia whispered to Jared, who was nodding his approval at them.

"They're submitting to him," he said, like he expected this all along. "Renewing their pledge to him as their alpha."

They are? Olivia watched in amazement as every single wolf in the room, even the Wildings in the corner, shifted and fell into the submission pose. Then Jared and his mother shifted as well. Only Jace and Jaxson were left standing in human form next to Olivia.

"It's all right, Jace," Jaxson said with a small smile. "You'll always be my brother, pledge or no."

Jace's face was a picture of torment. "I wish you had told me," he said, voice rough. "I'm your *brother*. I could have helped you carry that burden."

Jaxson reached for him with both hands, holding tight onto his shoulders. "Jace, you had enough burdens of your own. You didn't need to carry mine."

Jace's expression twisted further, like he was trying to hold some emotion inside, then he grabbed Jaxson into a fierce hug. Jaxson held onto him just as hard. When they broke apart, Jace held his brother's gaze for a long moment… then he knelt at his brother's feet and bowed his head. But he stayed in his human form.

Olivia wasn't sure what that meant—but at least he wasn't objecting anymore.

Jaxson quickly shifted to his wolf form, like the others, only he stood tall, ears perked, tail held high. His shiny black fur bristled out like a wave of static electricity had charged it. And then the strangest thing happened… *Olivia felt it too.* An echo of the magic that was charging Jaxson's wolf form swept through her, head to toe, and back again. It warmed every part of her, lifted her, made her feel… *loved.* Like she belonged. *At home.*

It was the most amazing, wondrous feeling, she couldn't keep the tears from coursing down her face.

Then one of the wolves yipped, and in one flow of fur and movement, they charged out of the great room, brushing against Olivia and Jaxson, still in his wolf form, as they went. While they cleared out, Jace rose from his spot in front of Jaxson and turned to Olivia.

"Of the three brothers," Jace said, his voice still rough with emotion, "you healed the one who deserved it the most." He swallowed, then added quietly. "Thank you for that."

Olivia smiled through her tears but didn't trust herself to say anything.

Jace ducked his head and loped out the front door, after the rest of his pack.

By the time she looked back to Jaxson, he had shifted to human form… only he was crouched on the floor, searching through the pile of clothes he left behind when he shifted.

He was truly a gorgeous man. Shifter enhanced muscles rippled over every inch of his body. It was marked with all the scars of the battles he'd endured… and she looked forward to exploring each and every one with her fingers and her kiss. Somehow the impossible had happened—she had embraced her witching side, she had gorgeous man who wanted her, and most miraculous of all, she had been accepted into a brand new, boisterous family of some of the finest people she'd ever known.

Jaxson finally stopped fussing with his clothes and stood up before her, completely naked. Olivia let her gaze travel the length of his ridiculously hot body. From the tattoo across his chest—*omni tempore,* all the time—down to his growing erection. Which just made her mouth water with anticipation.

She forced herself to drag her eyes up to meet his. "Please tell me you're dragging me off to the bridal suite." Her body was still radiating magical warmth from the bonding he performed with his pack, but just looking at Jaxson's sexy body was enough to heat every part of her.

He smirked. "Oh yes, Miss Lilyfield. But first, I have a question for you."

"Whatever it is, the answer is *yes, please God, yes.*"

He laughed, and that smile on his face was worth everything in the world to her. It *mattered* in a way nothing else ever had.

"You might want to hear the question first."

She shrugged one shoulder. "Details."

The smile was broad on his face as he stepped closer. Then he dropped to one knee and produced something shiny and small from behind his back. It took her a moment to realize it was a ring—silver twisted into the shape of claws holding a deep blue sapphire.

Her eyes went wide. *Was he—*

"Olivia Lilyfield, would you do me the honor of becoming my wife?"

She gasped. Her hands flew to cover her mouth. They trembled against her face. She was already bound by magic to him. He had already made her his mate. But for some reason, lost in all the extraordinary magic, she never expected this simple, *human* magic to ever be hers.

A lump the size of a baseball was stuck in her throat.

His grin was mischievous and loving and everything *Jaxson*. "You *promised* to say yes."

Her hands flew away from her face. *"Yes!"* Then she threw her arms around his neck, clinging to him and shedding her tears across his skin.

He held her for a moment, then gently pulled her away and slipped the ring on her finger. "Now," he said with a wicked sexy grin, "I'll try to work on that *yes, please God, yes* part."

Then he scooped her up in his arms and carried her away toward the bridal suite. It seemed impossible, but Jaxson River wanted to love her senseless for the rest of her life. And this brave and beautiful man never stopped until he got what he wanted. She could hardly believe that thing was *her*... but she would do everything in her power to keep that smile on his face forever.

Want more River brothers?
JACE (River Pack Wolves 2)

His wolf is out of control.
She's a wild thing that won't be tamed.
Get JACE today!

Subscribe to Alisa's newsletter to know when a new book is coming out!
http://smarturl.it/AWsubscribeBARDS

ABOUT THE AUTHOR

Alisa Woods lives in the Midwest with her husband and family, but her heart will always belong to the beaches and mountains where she grew up. She writes sexy paranormal romances about alpha men and the women who love them. She enjoys exploring the struggles we all have, where we resist—and succumb to—our most tempting vices as well as our greatest desires. She firmly believes that love triumphs over all.

All of Alisa's romances feature sexy alphas and the strong women who love them.

CPSIA information can be obtained
at www.ICGtesting.com
Printed in the USA
BVHW081948050822
643909BV00007B/402

9 781545 190555